You're holding in your hands a book that began as a paperback from one of many well-known publishers. Demco Media engineered it into a Turtleback®—a hardcover paperback built to withstand the rigors of exuberant young readers and dropbox circulation, but priced below the publisher's hardcover.

- Notice how the cover is constructed of high-density board and reinforced with either standard or library corners.
- Run your hands across the pressure-embossed satin finish—it reduces glare, avoids fingerprints, and resists spills and stains.
- And see how the top and bottom of the spine—the greatest points of wear—are reinforced with Tyvek,® a high-density polyethylene fiber that is extremely tear-resistant. A Turtleback exclusive!

A Turtleback is designed with young readers in mind.

- Children are attracted to the colorful graphics, which remain true to the publisher's original artwork.
- The bold lettering on the spine assures good readability on the shelf.
- And it won't "mousetrap shut" to frustrate a youngster—it's engineered to lie flat, fully exposing inside margins.

Known as a "prebound" in the industry, a Turtleback is quite simply the best hardcover paperback that money can buy. That's why we're proud to say: **If you're not completely satisfied with any Turtleback Book at any time, for any reason, call our toll-free number (800) 448-8939 and we'll either replace it, issue a credit, or send you a prompt refund.**

Contact Demco Media for Your Free Master Catalog / CD

Call (800) 448-8939
Fax (800) 828-0401
Web www.turtlebackbooks.com
Mail Demco Media, P.O. Box 14260, Madison, WI 53714-0260

RANDOM HOUSE
CHILDREN'S BOOKS
A DIVISION OF RANDOM HOUSE, INC.

Dear Educator:

We are pleased to send you our most recent teacher's edition—and something that's a departure for us. This book includes a selection from four award-winning middle-grade novels, along with teacher's guides to extend the curriculum use of each. From speaking with many of you at conferences, we know how much you enjoy sharing new and interesting fiction with your students. So we have selected excerpts from some of our best new novels for you to experience together.

Our sampler begins with Kimberly Willis Holt's National Book Award winner, *When Zachary Beaver Came to Town*. Set in Texas during the summer of 1971, it tells of friendship in a small town and how the arrival of an outsider brings upheaval, havoc, humor, and redemption.

Those of you who have read Ms. Holt in the past and enjoyed her luminous storytelling style will not be disappointed in this recent work!

Our other three novels move through the Civil War, World War I, and the Great Depression. (See next page.) But just as *Zachary Beaver* is more than a story about America during the Vietnam War, these works of historical fiction are more, too, as they explore the powerful themes of friendship, self-discovery, and children's courageous choices in times of great upheaval.

I hope that you will share this edition with your students and colleagues. I also hope that you will return the enclosed comment card so that we can continue to do our very best for you. I look forward to hearing from you.

Sincerely,

Sharon K. Hancock

Sharon K. Hancock
Associate Director
School & Library Marketing

ALFRED A. KNOPF BOOKS FOR YOUNG READERS • BANTAM BOOKS FOR YOUNG READERS • CROWN BOOKS FOR YOUNG READERS • CTW BOOKS • DRAGONFLY BOOKS
DELACORTE PRESS BOOKS FOR YOUNG READERS • DOUBLEDAY BOOKS FOR YOUNG READERS • LAUREL-LEAF BOOKS • RANDOM HOUSE BOOKS FOR YOUNG READERS • YEARLING BOOKS

1540 BROADWAY, NEW YORK, NY 10036 • TELEPHONE 212.782.9000

CONTENTS

When Zachary Beaver Came to Town
by Kimberly Willis Holt

Summer Soldiers
by Susan Hart Lindquist

Three Against the Tide
by D. Anne Love

A Letter to Mrs. Roosevelt
by C. Coco De Young

RANDOM HOUSE
CHILDREN'S BOOKS
A DIVISION OF RANDOM HOUSE, INC.

PRAISE FOR

When Zachary Beaver Came to Town

★ "In her own down-to-earth, people-smart way, Holt offers a gift. . . . It is a lovely—at times even giddy—date with real life." —Starred, *The Horn Book Magazine*

★ "As in her first novel, *My Louisiana Sky*, Holt humanizes the outsider without sentimentality. . . . In the tradition of many Southern writers, Holt reveals the freak in all of us, and the power of redemption." — Starred, *Booklist*

★ "A master at finding the extraordinary in the ordinary . . . [Holt] breath[es] life into a quirky cast of characters. The characters tug at readers, gaining steadily their attention and affection." —Starred, *Kirkus Reviews*

America Honors *When Zachary Beaver Came to Town*

A National Book Award Winner
An ALA Best Book for Young Adults
An ALA Notable Children's Book
A *Booklist* Editors' Choice
A *School Library Journal* Best Book of the Year

When Zachary Beaver Came to Town

KIMBERLY WILLIS HOLT

A YEARLING BOOK

Published by
Dell Yearling
an imprint of
Random House Children's Books
a division of Random House, Inc.
1540 Broadway
New York, New York 10036

To order classroom sets of *When Zachary Beaver Came to Town*
in paperback, please contact your local distributor or bookstore.

The paperback edition
(ISBN 0-440-22904-9)
will be available in April 2001.

Promotional copy—not for sale

Visit us on the Web! www.randomhouse.com/kids

**Educators and librarians, for a variety of teaching tools, visit us at
www.randomhouse.com/teachers**

ISBN: 0-440-22904-9

Reprinted by arrangement with Henry Holt and Company, LLC

Printed in the United States of America

April 2001

OPM

For
Christy Ottaviano
and
Jennifer Flannery

Chapter One

Nothing ever happens in Antler, Texas. Nothing much at all. Until this afternoon, when an old blue Thunderbird pulls a trailer decorated with Christmas lights into the Dairy Maid parking lot. The red words painted on the trailer cause quite a buzz around town, and before an hour is up, half of Antler is standing in line with two dollars clutched in hand to see the fattest boy in the world.

Since it's too late in the summer for firecrackers and too early for the Ladybug Waltz, Cal and I join Miss Myrtie Mae and the First Baptist Quilting Bee at the back of the line.

Miss Myrtie Mae wears a wide-brimmed straw hat. She claims that she's never exposed her skin to sun. Even so, wrinkles fold into her face like an unironed shirt. She takes her job as town historian and librarian seriously, and as usual, her camera hangs around her neck. "Toby, how's your mom?"

"Fine," I say.

"That will really be something if she wins."

"Yes, ma'am, it will." My mouth says the words, but my mind is not wanting to settle on a picture of her winning. Mom dreams of following in the footsteps of her favorite singer, Tammy Wynette. Last month she entered a singing contest in Amarillo and won first place. She got a trophy and an all-expense-paid trip to Nashville for a week to enter the National Amateurs' Country Music Competition at the Grand Ole Opry. The winner gets to cut a record album.

Cars and pickups pull into the Dairy Maid parking lot. Some people make no bones about it. They just get in line to see him. Others try to act like they don't know anything about the buzz. They enter the Dairy Maid, place their orders, and exit with Coke floats, chocolate-dipped cones, or curlicue fries, then wander to the back of the line. They don't fool me.

The line isn't moving because the big event hasn't started. Some skinny guy wearing a tuxedo, smoking a pipe, is taking the money and giving out green tickets. Cal could stand in line forever to relieve his curiosity. He knows more gossip than any old biddy in Antler because he gathers it down at the cotton gin, where his dad and the other farmers drink coffee.

"I got better things to do than this," I tell Cal. Like eat. My stomach's been growling all the time now because I haven't had a decent meal since Mom left a few days ago. Not that she cooked much lately since she was getting ready for that stupid contest. But I miss the fried catfish and barbecue dinners she brought home from the Bowl-a-Rama Cafe, where she works.

"Oh, come on, Toby," Cal begs. "He'll probably move out tomorrow and we'll never get another chance."

"He's just some fat kid. Heck, Malcolm Clifton probably has him beat hands down." Malcolm's mom claims he's big boned, not fat, but we've seen him pack away six jumbo burgers. I sigh real big like my dad does when he looks at my report card filled with Cs. "Okay," I say. "But I'm only waiting ten more minutes. After that, I'm splitting."

Cal grins that stupid grin with his black tooth showing. He likes to brag that he got his black tooth playing football, but I know the real story. His sister, Kate, socked him good when he scratched up her Carole King album. Cal says he was sick of hearing "You Make Me Feel Like a Natural Woman" every stinking day of his life.

Scarlett Stalling walks toward the line, holding her bratty sister Tara's hand. Scarlett looks cool wearing a bikini top underneath an open white blouse and hip huggers that hit right below her belly button. With her golden tan and long, silky blond hair, she could do a commercial for Coppertone.

Scarlett doesn't go to the back of the line. She walks over to me. *To me.* Smiling, flashing that Ultra Brite sex appeal smile and the tiny gap between her two front teeth. Cal grins, giving her the tooth, but I lower my eyelids half-mast and jerk my head back a little as if to say, "Hey."

Then she speaks. "Hey, Toby, would y'all do me a favor?"

"Sure," I squeak, killing my cool act in one split second.

Scarlett flutters her eyelashes, and I suck in my breath. "Take Tara in for me." She passes her little sister's sticky hand like she's handing over a dog's leash. Then she squeezes her fingers into her pocket and pulls out two crumpled dollar bills. I would give anything to be one of those lucky dollar bills tucked into her pocket.

She flips back her blond mane. "I've got to get back home and get ready. Juan's dropping by soon."

The skin on my chest prickles. Mom is right. Scarlett Stalling is a flirt. Mom always told me, "You better stay a spittin' distance from that girl. Her mother had a bad reputation when I went to school, and the apple doesn't fall far from the tree."

Cal punches my shoulder. "Great going, ladies' man!"

I watch Scarlett's tight jeans sway toward her house so she can get ready for the only Mexican guy in Antler Junior High. Juan already shaves. He's a head taller than the rest of the guys (two heads taller than me). That gives him an instant ticket to play first string on our basketball team, even though he's slow footed and a lousy shot. Whenever I see him around town, a number-five-iron golf club swings at his side. I don't plan to ever give him a reason to use it.

"Fatty, fatty, two by four," Tara chimes as she stares at the trailer. "Can't get through the kitchen door."

"Shut up, squirt," I mutter.

Miss Myrtie Mae frowns at me.

Tara yanks on my arm. "Uummmm!" she hollers. "You said shut up. Scarlett!" She rises on her toes as if that makes her louder. "Toby said shut up to me!"

But it's too late. Scarlett has already disappeared across the street. She's probably home smearing gloss on those pouty lips while I hold her whiny sister's lollipop fingers, standing next to my black-toothed best friend, waiting to see the fattest boy in the world.

Chapter Two

There's not a cloud in the sky, and it's boiling hot. Wylie Womack's snow cone stand is across the parking lot, under the giant elm tree, and the idea is real tempting to let go of Tara's hand and bolt for it. But that would kill any chance I would ever have with Scarlett.

Sheriff Levi Fetterman drives by, making his afternoon rounds. He slows down and looks our way. His riding dog, Duke, sits in the passenger seat. Duke is Sheriff Levi's favorite adoptee. Anytime someone in Antler finds a stray cat or dog, they call the sheriff to pick up the animal and take it to the pound. Sheriff Levi can't bear to dump a dog, and because of that he has a couple dozen living on his one-acre place a mile out of town. However, cats are a different story. They go straight to the pound.

Sheriff Levi waves at us, then heads on his way. He drives all the way down Main Street and turns toward the highway.

Finally the skinny guy selling tickets moves to the top step in front of the trailer door. Even though he smokes a pipe, his baby face, braces, and tux make him look like he's ready for the eighth-grade formal. From the front his hair looks short, but he turns and I notice a ponytail hangs down his back.

"Welcome, fine folks," he yells like a carnival barker. His voice is older than his face—deep and clear like a DJ's. "Step this way to see Zachary Beaver, the fattest boy in the world. Six hundred and forty-three pounds. You don't have to rush, but keep in mind others behind you want a look too. My name is Paulie Rankin, and I'll be happy to take your questions."

"And your money too," Cal says out of the corner of his mouth. "By the way, can you loan me two bucks?" I nod and peel two dollars from my wallet.

Tara jumps and jumps. "I can't wait! I can't wait! Do you think he's fatter than Santa?"

"How would I know?" I grumble.

Cal kneels next to her. "I'll bet he's three times fatter than Santa."

Her eyes grow big. "Oooh! That's *real* fat."

Cal likes little kids, but then, he sometimes acts

like one. Maybe because he's the youngest in the family. He has two brothers and one sister. His oldest brother, Wayne, is in the army, serving in Vietnam. He's the kind of big brother I wish I had.

Wayne writes to Cal every week. But Cal is so lazy, he hardly ever writes him back. If I had a brother in Vietnam that wrote me letters saying what a neat brother I was, I'd always write him back.

Cal reads every letter to me. Wayne never says anything about the kind of stuff we see on the news—no blood and guts. He writes about home. How he misses lying in bed, listening to Casey Kasem and Wolfman Jack on the radio. How he wishes he could eat a Bahama Mama snow cone from Wylie Womack's stand and let the syrup run down his fingers. And how the worst day of his life, before he got drafted, was the day he missed catching that fly ball during the Bucks-Cardinals game because he was too busy watching some girl walk up the stands in her pink hot pants. He says he'd live that day over a hundred times if it meant he could come back home. Wayne makes Antler sound like the best place on the face of the earth. Sometimes he even adds: *P.S. Tell your buddy Toby I said hey*.

The line moves slowly, and when people exit the trailer, some come out all quiet like they've been shaken up at a revival. A few say things like, "Lord-a-mercy!" Others joke and laugh.

Finally we make it to the front door. I hand Paulie Rankin four bucks and glance down at Tara. Legs crossed, she's bouncing like crazy.

Paulie pulls the pipe out of his mouth. "Hey, the kid doesn't have to *go*, does she?"

"Do you?" I ask her, not intending to sound as mean as it comes out.

She shakes her head, making her two tiny blond ponytails flop like puppy ears.

"She better not," says Paulie. He rubs his chin and watches her suspiciously as we climb the trailer steps.

I grit my teeth and repeat Paulie's warning. "You better not."

The cramped trailer smells like Pine-Sol and lemon Pledge and it's dark except for a lamp and sunlight slipping between the crack in the curtains. A drape hangs at one end, hiding the space behind it. And in the middle of the trailer sits the largest human being I've ever seen. Zachary Beaver is the size of a two-man pup tent. His short black hair tops his huge moon face like a snug cap that's two sizes too small. His skin is pale as buttermilk, and his hazel eyes are practically lost in his puffy cheeks.

Wearing huge pull-on pants and a brown T-shirt, he sits in front of a television, watching *Password*, drinking a giant chocolate milk shake. A *TV Guide* rests on his lap, and a few stacks of books and *Newsweek* magazines are at his feet along with a sack of Lay's potato chips. Three Plexiglas walls box him in. The walls aren't very high, but I figure they keep brats like Tara from poking him. After all, he's not the Pillsbury Doughboy. A sign in the corner of one wall reads, Don't Touch the Glass, but if someone does, a squirt bottle of glass cleaner and a roll of paper towels are next to the TV.

There's no denying it—this place is clean with a capital *C*. And with the exception of a dusty bookcase filled with encyclopedias and other books, it's as sterile as a hospital. A gold cardboard box is on the center shelf by itself.

It seems weird, standing here, staring at someone because they look different. Wylie Womack is the strangest-looking person in Antler, but I'm so used to seeing his crooked body riding around town in his beat-up golf cart that I don't think about him looking weird.

Miss Myrtie Mae steps forward, lifting her camera. "Mind if I take a few pictures?"

"Yes, I do," the fat kid says.

Miss Myrtie Mae lets the camera drop to her chest. "You like books, I see. I work at the Antler library."

Zachary Beaver ignores her.

For once Tara is quiet, but Cal is anything but speechless. He wants to know everything. Like a red-headed woodpecker, he *pecks, pecks, pecks*, trying to make a dent.

"How much do you eat?" he asks Zachary.

"As much as I can."

"How old are you?"

"Old enough."

"Where do you go to school?"

"You're looking at it." Zachary never once smiles or looks us in the eye. He focuses on that game show.

Then Cal asks, "What's in the gold box?"

Zachary ignores him, his gaze dragging across Cal's face.

I wish Cal would shut up. Besides embarrassing me, his questions sound mean. But Zachary only looks bored and kind of irritated, like someone swishing away a fly.

I don't ask questions, but I think them. Like how did he get inside the trailer? He's way too wide to fit through the door. Tara's stupid chant plays over and over in my mind. *Fatty, fatty, two by four. Can't get through the kitchen door.* I'm surprised she hasn't started singing it. I look down at her. Her bugged-out eyes water, and one hand covers her mouth. The other is locked between her crossed legs. A yellow stream trickles down her leg and wets her white Keds.

I jump back. "Jeez—!"

Zachary looks up from the TV, his eyes flashing, his wide nostrils flaring. "Do I smell pee? Did that kid pee in here?" He points toward the exit, the flesh on his arm flapping as he punches his finger in the air. "Get her outta here!"

Every eye in the trailer stares at us. Except Cal, who is snooping around, picking up stuff. I want to yank Tara by her ponytails, punt her like a football, and send her sailing through the air, across the street, toward her house to knock down Juan as he arrives at Scarlett's door. Instead I grab Tara by the hand—the one that covers her mouth—and whip through the exit, past the waiting crowd. Taking long strides so that Tara must run to keep from falling, I cross two streets to her house, where Juan sits on the left side of the porch swing, holding Scarlett's hand. His number-five iron is at his feet, and he wears a white T-shirt with *Don't Mess with Super Mex* printed in ink across the front.

"He was soooo fat!" yells Tara, running inside their

13

house. A great big wet spot covers the rear end of her shorts.

This has got to be my lowest moment ever. I swerve around, trying to avoid Juan and Scarlett.

But it's too late. Juan calls out, "Hey, man, I didn't know you baby-sat."

Chapter Three

Seeing Scarlett and Juan together rattles me so bad, I almost forget my bike parked in front of the Dairy Maid. By the time I get back, the line has died down and Cal is gone. I hop on my bike, ride past the town square, and head home.

Antler is off Highway 287, tucked between the railroad tracks and the breaks of Palo Duro Canyon. Because of the breaks, it's not as flat and sparse as most of the Panhandle. Most Panhandle towns don't have trees unless someone planted them, but Antler has plenty of elms and cedars.

Our town's population has been shrinking since the bank foreclosed on some of the farms. A lot of the stores are vacant. Ferris Kelly's Bowl-a-Rama, Earline's Real Estate Agency, and Clifton's Dry Goods remain. Antique shops started opening in some of the vacant stores a couple of years ago.

The majority of the people who shop at the antique stores are passing through from Fort Worth or Dallas. Which is weird because they look like they can afford new stuff.

A cotton gin sits at the outskirts of Antler, and it isn't unusual to see a speck of cotton surfing on the wind like a lost snowflake.

Our house on Ivy Street is four streets away from the square and two streets from the school. Even though Cal's family owns a cotton farm on the edge of town, they live next door to us in a small brick house. It doesn't seem fair—Cal's family stuffed in their little place like sardines while the three of us live in a big two-story.

Not that our house is a mansion or anything. Mom calls it a hand-me-down. First it belonged to Mom's grandparents, then her parents, now us. It looks like the kind of place you'd see on a farm surrounded by acres of land—a white clapboard with a wraparound porch and a weather vane on the roof.

When I reach home, I see Cal's bike lying flat in his yard. His brother Billy is working on Wayne's old Mustang in their driveway. He's trying to get it fixed up to surprise Wayne when he comes home in March.

A flag waves from a tall pole in their front yard. Before Wayne went to Vietnam, they only hung it on the Fourth of July and other patriotic holidays. Now the flag goes up every morning and comes down each night.

Cal's mom, Mrs. McKnight, is pruning her roses in their front yard while she hums a song. I listen close, but I don't know the tune. Maybe it's an old Irish song. Cal says his mom's family passed them down like an old quilt.

As usual, Mrs. McKnight wears a floral apron tied around her waist. She's the only one in Cal's family who isn't redheaded. Right now her black hair blows wildly in the breeze. It makes me think how Mom puts so much hair spray on hers it defies any Panhandle wind and teases it so high it could hide a Frisbee. Mom claims big hair helps her hit the high notes.

Mrs. McKnight waves, and I wave back. "Any word from your mom?"

"Not yet." I wish everyone would stop asking me about Mom. She only left a few days ago, and the contest isn't until next Thursday. After Thursday they'll ask, "How did she do?" At least that fat guy replaced Mom as the juiciest news in town.

At home, Mozart plays from the stereo while Dad stands at the sink, slicing bell peppers. He's wearing his post office uniform with his black Bic pens neatly lined up in his shirt pocket. His head is bent, and I notice his bald spot has grown to the size of an orange. Radishes, onions, and lettuce from his backyard garden lie on the counter. Dad's fingers are long and straight. As postmaster he sorts mail at the post office as quick as a card shark deals out a deck. But right now, cutting those peppers, his fingers look clumsy and awkward. "Hungry?" he asks.

"Yeah, I guess."

"I thought I'd make a salad." Dad may grow the vegetables, but he's never made a salad in his life. He looks lost in the kitchen, digging around for a salad bowl. He opens a cabinet, scratches his chin, then selects another door. I don't know where to find a bowl either. I search in the pantry. The shelves are filled with food. Boxes of cereal, pasta, and crackers, cans of soup, stewed tomatoes, and green peas. I open the refrigerator. Milk, eggs, and American cheese slices are jammed next to packages of ham and bologna. Dad always griped at the way Mom never kept enough groceries in the house. Now she's prepared us for a national disaster.

All that food reminds me of the night she packed for her trip. I sat on the edge of her bed, watching her. Every pair of cowboy boots she owned lined the wall, including the turquoise ones with red stars. She flung all her western shirts and skirts on the bed and dropped lipstick tubes from under her sink into a small suitcase. I swear she packed like she was going for the whole summer instead of a week. About the only thing she didn't pack was the pearl necklace that once belonged to her mom. She told me that someday she'd give it to the woman I married so it would stay in the family. Mom sang "Hey, Good Lookin' " as she packed, and the entire time I couldn't help wondering if moms were supposed to be that happy to get away. Mrs. McKnight doesn't go on trips without her family.

Dad has already set the table with Mom's vinyl Las Vegas show scene place mats. Elvis in a white glittered suit looks up at me, microphone in hand. The table seems enormous without Mom sitting at her place. And it's quiet. Mom did all the talking at dinner. While Dad and I ate, she'd tell us something funny the Judge, Miss Myrtie Mae's senile brother, said that day at the cafe. Or how Sheriff Levi finally ordered something different from the menu, only to quickly change it back to his usual—hamburger with jalapeños and French fries.

I always knew Mom dreamed of being a famous singer, but I guess I thought it was only a dream. The kind of thing you wish for upon a star, but deep down you know it probably won't ever come true. After all, stars are a long ways away.

Dad's salad really isn't bad if you take out the onions. They smell strong, but I eat around them. He looks like he's waiting for me to mention the salad, so I tell him, "Pretty good, Dad."

"Really?" He sounds relieved, and I'm glad I said something.

"Yeah."

"I didn't use too many onions?"

I look down at the sliced onions around the edge of my plate. "Well, I've never been crazy about onions anyway."

"I'll try and remember next time."

I want to say, Don't sweat it, Dad. Mom will be back soon enough. No need turning into a gourmet chef.

Dad might as well be from Pluto as from Dallas. People in Antler see it as the same thing. The funny thing is, now it seems like Dad belongs here more than Mom. I don't think she ever counted on him settling in Antler when he passed through years ago, looking for a place to raise worms.

Dad is the Otto Wilson part of Otto Wilson's Tennessee Brown Nose Fishing Worms. He keeps most of the bait shops stocked from here to Lake Kiezer and Lake Seymour. He also raises enough for the local men heading out to their favorite fishing holes. I help take care of the worms—separating them by size, changing their soil and keeping it moist.

After dinner Dad and I do the dishes while we listen to the television news. We stand side by side; I barely reach his shoulder. People say I take after Mom—blond, brown eyed, and *small*.

When the war correspondent comes on, the volume gets louder. The reporter hollers into his microphone, trying to be heard over the sounds of helicopters and M-16s in the background.

Dad turns around and glances at the television screen. "Turn that crap off, will you?"

As I walk toward the TV, I wonder if Wayne is there or someplace like it.

Later I ride my bike past the town limits to Gossimer Lake. Dusk has arrived, and even though the sun is sinking below the horizon, I can see the moon. I pass the Dairy Maid, where the crowd has left. Now that it's dark, the Christmas lights glow like fallen stars strung around the trailer. Paulie Rankin sits outside his Thunderbird in a lawn chair, smoking his pipe and gazing up at the sky. I guess he'll head out in the morning to the next town full of suckers with two dollars to burn.

What a sorry life Zachary Beaver must have, sitting every day in a cramped trailer while people come by to gawk at him. But at least he goes places. At least he doesn't watch the girl of his dreams hold hands with some other guy or have a mom who's off becoming Tammy Wynette. Except for having Cal, life in Antler is about as exciting as watching worms mate. And Cal can be such a dork. He may be the reason I'm batting a big fat zero with Scarlett. Maybe he's ruining my image.

Gossimer Lake is more like a large pond. It started out as a puny mud puddle. One spring we had an unusual amount of rain, and a mud puddle on Henrick Gossimer's land grew to the size of a kiddie pool. Mr. Gossimer said he thought it was the Lord's way of saying he should do something for Antler's young folks. He dug the ground around the puddle as much as he could, then he called on Mr. Owens to bulldoze the rest.

Pretty soon it became a town project. The First Baptist men's group built a small dam to keep in the water, and the Shriners club raised a windmill to keep the lake filled. That's how dried-up Antler got its man-made lake. It's about as good as a mud puddle, though. Signs posted everywhere read, No Swimming. No Fishing. They might as well post one that reads, No Fun Allowed.

I dodge the trees that fringe the lake, jump off my

bike, and flop on the grass near the edge of the water. A light breeze blows from the southwest, bringing the stink of the Martins' cattle feedlot. I take off my sneakers and socks and roll up my jeans. Once Cal and I waded into the water, but when Cal said, "I wonder if there's any snakes in here?" I jumped out and he quickly followed. Tonight I don't care if a snake pit is at the bottom of this giant puddle. Let them bite.

Just as I step into the water, I hear grass rustle and I decide maybe I'm not sold on seeing a snake after all. Across the lake, two figures sit close to each other. One of them moves, and I see a glimmer of blond hair. My stomach feels sick as my eyes zero in on Scarlett and Juan.

Chapter Four

The next morning I jolt from a deep sleep. Dirt clods thump against my bedroom window, and Cal is calling my name. When I pull up my shade, light spills into the room. I have to squint real hard to see Cal looking up at me from the ground.

"Come on!" he hollers. "You going to sleep all day?"

It's only eight in the morning. With Cal McKnight as my best friend, I don't need an alarm clock. His family has a morning routine. Everyone up by 6 A.M., no matter if it's summer—beds made, breakfast eaten, dishes washed and put away, teeth brushed by six-thirty, then on to the chore list attached to the refrigerator with a smiley face magnet. The list has three columns, with each McKnight kid's name (except Wayne's) at the top—Kate, Billy, and Cal. Whenever I spend the night with Cal, I get thrown into their routine. But I don't mind. They seem like a happy army on a mission, zipping through their list.

In the summer they're out the door by eight, with hoes in their hands, headed to work in their cotton field. Most of the cotton farmers use herbicide to control weeds and insecticide to get rid of the bugs. Except for releasing the ladybugs in his fields once a year, Mr. McKnight doesn't use anything. He believes a penny saved is a penny earned.

Once Mom looked out the kitchen window and shook her head when she saw Cal, Kate, and Cal's brothers piling into the back of the pickup with their tools. "Charlie McKnight works his kids like slaves. He has hired help to do that." Mom believes a penny earned is a penny spent at Clifton's Dry Goods.

But today is Saturday, and even Cal's dad gives his kids the weekend off. I yawn, stretch, and tell Cal to wait. Then I straighten the green plastic soldiers lined up on my dresser and cross yesterday off the calendar. Two hundred thirty-one more days until Wayne comes home. After stumbling into a T-shirt and jeans, I grab two English muffins and go outside. I need to wet down the worms' dirt, but Dad won't mind if I do it later as long as it's done today.

Cal waits on his bike, hands gripping the handlebars

so tight, his knuckles turn white. "Hey, snoozer, what took you so long?"

I ignore him, toss him a muffin, and head to the garage to get my own bike. Next door, Kate tries to parallel park the McKnight station wagon between two garbage cans set on the street. She looks like an old lady—frizzy red hair twisted in a knot on top of her head, glasses low on her nose, shoulders hiked up to her ears, and her body curled over the steering wheel.

Every high school junior in Antler already has their driver's license except for Kate. Mrs. McKnight drove her to Amarillo three times this summer to take the test, and each time Kate failed the driving part because she can't parallel park. Now she frantically looks from the rearview mirror to the side mirror, inching the car backward.

Watching from my driveway, Cal and I straddle our bikes and eat our dry muffins. I stop chewing. I even cross my fingers, wanting for her to succeed this time. But as usual, she backs into the rear garbage can, knocking it over, causing the metal to clank against the road.

"Oh!" Cal smacks his hands against his chest and falls off his bike in slow motion. "She got me, buddy."

Flat on his back, the rear tire covering his legs, he raises his head and looks her way. I laugh.

Kate jumps out of the station wagon, pushes up her glasses, and returns the can to its upright position. Her baggy jeans and tie-dyed T-shirt swallow her skinny body. Before getting back behind the wheel, she faces Cal, tight fists at her sides, and glares.

"Come on," Cal says. "Let's get out of here before she blows."

We race down the sidewalks on Ivy Street, Cal on the right side of the road, me on the left. We jump curbs like track stars leaping hurdles. We take sharp turns at the corner of Ivy and Langston, leaning into the wind, knowing we won't fall because we've done it a million times before. We can stop our bikes on a dime, and we do when we reach the school. In a few months the grounds will be crawling with kids, but right now Malcolm is mowing it with his dad's riding mower. From the looks of it, he's been at it awhile, and the smell of freshly cut grass floats in the air. He waves and we wave back, but Cal yells, "Hey, Malcolm. You big goofball! Crybaby!"

We're safe because Malcolm can't hear Cal through the motor's growl. He waves again, sucks in his big gut, and accelerates like he's on a Harley-Davidson.

He's wearing his Antler Wrestling T-shirt, but the only wrestling action Malcolm has seen is from the bench.

Last summer the three of us were out by Sheriff Levi's place with the electric fence surrounding it. Cal and I challenged Malcolm to a pissing contest. We stood facing the fence, only Cal and I undershot. As we predicted, show-off Malcolm aimed for the fence, and as soon as he successfully hit his target, he was knocked flat on his back. It didn't really hurt him, but the shock shook him up bad. He had hollered, "A snake! I got bit by a snake!" Cal and I split a gut laughing, but Malcolm ran home crying to his mother. We were grounded for weeks.

"How much do you think that guy eats?" Cal asks.

"Malcolm?" I ask.

"No," Cal says, shaking his head. "Zachary Beaver."

"He told you. As much as he can."

"Man, that guy was huge," Cal continues. "I wonder if he's in the *Guinness Book of World Records*."

"Who cares?"

"Do you think he really weighs 643 pounds?"

I shrug. "I don't know. I guess."

"I mean, how do they weigh him? Most scales don't go that high."

"Maybe they weigh him at a meat market."

Cal scratches his chin. "I wonder how he goes to the bathroom?"

"How do *you* go to the bathroom?"

"You know what I mean. I mean, does he have to have a special toilet?"

I roll my eyes.

"And what do you think he keeps in that gold cardboard box?"

I don't want to talk about the fat kid. It makes my stomach ache because it reminds me of what happened with Tara, and that reminds me of seeing Scarlett and Juan at the lake last night.

"Where to now?" I ask.

"How about Wylie's?"

"It's too early for a snow cone," I say. "Besides, he doesn't open until one."

"Swimming?"

I throw him a steely gaze. He knows better. I haven't been swimming at the town pool since last summer, when I swallowed a bunch of pool water and started choking. The lifeguard got excited and yanked me out of the pool and did mouth-to-mouth resuscitation.

"Oh, yeah," Cal remembers. "Bowling?"

"I guess." Nothing sounds particularly fun this morning. The wind has started to kick up, and Cal's red curls blow around his face.

"Did your mom win?"

"For the hundredth time, the contest isn't until next Thursday night."

"You got cash?" Cal asks, not a bit embarrassed.

"Some. Not enough for both of us."

"Then I better stop home first. Sure hope Kate has cooled off."

"You're going to hit her up for money?"

"Have to. Billy is as broke as me. He sinks every penny he makes at the drive-in into Wayne's old junker. Kate saves money like Scrooge."

"Man, you're brave."

Cal never has money with him. He usually bums some off me, then forgets to pay me back. One day when I was mad at him, I added up every single cent I loaned him since fifth grade. Forty-six bucks. We made up the next day, so I never told him.

When we return, the McKnights' station wagon is parked in the driveway and the garbage cans are gone. Inside their house, the *Sound of Music* album plays in the background. Next to Carole King, Kate likes show tunes best.

Kate hunches over her sewing machine at the

dining-room table. Billy sleeps on the couch, oblivious to the music and the growl of the machine.

Cal walks over to Kate and grabs a piece of blue shiny fabric pinned to a pattern section on the table.

"Put that down!" she snaps.

Holding the piece to his chest, he skips around the room like a sissy, singing with the music, "I am sixteen going on seventeen." It would have been funny except Kate didn't deserve it. I want to tell her—I'm not like him. I think he's acting like a jerk too.

Kate jumps to her feet, but her shoulders remain hunched. Her face tense, she pushes at the POW bracelets she wears on each arm. Most girls have only one. Not Kate. She says, if some guys are being held prisoner in Vietnam, the least she can do is wear their names on her wrists. "Put it down, Cal Michael McKnight, right this instant! Or else!"

Billy doesn't stir. He even starts to snore. I stand there, helpless. I dread these moments when Cal torments Kate for no reason. She really isn't all that bad.

Kate chases Cal and yanks the fabric out of his hand. The pattern rips and the fabric drops to the floor. Kate's eyes bulge. "Now look what you've done."

"Whoops," Cal says. "I guess this means you won't loan me three bucks."

She grabs the fabric off the ground. "Get out of this

house, Cal McKnight, or I'll throw you out on your skinny butt!"

Billy's eyes pop wide, and without bothering to find out why Kate's freaking out, he yells, "Get out, Cal. You punk!"

Cal pulls my shirt as he bolts from the room and heads for the front door. We hop on our bikes and pedal like crazy, the wind smacking our faces. We ride along in silence with only the sound of our tires meeting the pavement. From a distance, I hear the train pulling into the depot. "When are the ladybugs getting here?"

"Dad said probably next week sometime."

Last year the ladybugs arrived closer to the Fourth of July. Now I wonder if it will be too late for the ladybugs to get rid of the bollworms. I guess I'm excited because this will be the first year that Cal and I get to empty the sacks of ladybugs in the field. "Where to now?" I ask.

"Let's go to the Bowl-a-Rama." That's what's boring about living in Antler. There's only a handful of things to do, and when we don't have money for those things, we usually go anyway and watch other people do them.

The Bowl-a-Rama sits across the street from the Dairy Maid. As we approach, I'm surprised to see the trailer still parked in the lot. But this time something is missing—Paulie Rankin's blue Thunderbird.

Cal and I stop pedaling at the same time and stare at the trailer. "Maybe they went to another town to eat," I say.

"Do you think *he's* still there?" Cal asks. "I mean, the fat kid?"

"Nah," I say, but I wonder too. "Come on. It's too hot to stay out here." We park our bikes on the sidewalk and head inside.

The Bowl-a-Rama smells of sweaty feet and cigarettes, but it's the coldest place in town. Today the air conditioner is cranked so high, goose bumps pop out on my arms. Two of the six lanes broke last summer, but Ferris hasn't bothered to have them fixed.

Ferris leans against the counter, where the bowling shoes are kept, rubbing his long Elvis sideburns. With his shirtsleeves rolled up, his two tattoos are visible. One is an anchor, the other a hula girl. He said he got them the night he met Jim Beam. Cal thought he was talking about a real person until I explained that Jim Beam was whiskey and Ferris was drunk as a skunk when he got the tattoos. That was before Ferris met Jesus and got religion.

Ferris is staring out the window, and it takes him a

moment to recognize us. Finally he rubs his eyes with his thumb and finger. "Hey, fellas, if you stare into the sun too long, it'll blind ya." He yawns and scratches his day-old whiskers, making a *wisk-wisk* sound. "How's your mom, Toby?"

"Great." I guess.

"Well, the next time she calls, you tell her that her job is waiting for her. After all, where else can folks in Antler get a meal with free entertainment?"

Mom is known as the singing waitress. She makes up songs for the customers, and if they're a pain, she makes up songs *about* them. Her voice is high and strong with just the right twang. She may sing songs about honky-tonk angels while serving Bowl-a-Rama specials, but in her mind she's probably on the stage of the Grand Ole Opry.

In the cafe, next to the picture of the Lord's Supper, Ferris hung a huge banner above the soda fountain counter—Good Luck, Opalina!

Ferris comes out from behind the counter, limping to the door and turning the Open sign around to face the front. The talk around town is his limp was a self-inflicted wound so he didn't have to serve in the Korean War. Ferris claims it was a pure coincidence that he was cleaning his gun the day before he was to report for active duty.

Before that happened, Ferris wanted to be a preacher. He even went a semester to a Bible college in Oklahoma. Now he never goes to church, but Mom says he knows the Bible from Genesis to Revelation. It's almost as hard for me to picture Ferris a preacher as it is believing he'd ever ditch a war.

Cal hops on the counter. "What's up, Ferris?"

"Oh, nothing much in here. But I've been curious about what's going on across the street."

"How's that?" I prop my elbow on the counter and rest my chin on my fist.

"That freak show fella took off in his Thunderbird about an hour ago."

"Did the fat guy go with him?" Cal asks, hopping off the counter.

"Don't think so," Ferris says. "That's what's got me to wonderin'. Thought they'd be pulling out by now."

Cal heads for the door. He glances back and waves his arm in giant sweeps. "Come on."

Underneath the trailer, a hose and wire stretch across the parking lot to the inside of the Dairy Maid. Paulie Rankin must have worked out something for the electricity and water.

"Help me up," Cal says. And a minute later, Cal

sits on top of my shoulders, peeking through the crack between the drapes in the back window.

I get a weird feeling that maybe we shouldn't be doing this. My heart pounds like a ticking bomb.

"Cal, they arrest people for looking in windows. The fat kid could be taking a bath or something."

"Jeez!"

"The sheriff could drive by. He could slap handcuffs on us and haul our butts to the county jail."

"Mary, and Joseph!" Cal calls out.

My heart leaps into my throat, but I risk it and trade places with Cal to take a look.

It's the back of Zachary Beaver. Through the grimy streaked window, I watch him eating frosted corn-flakes from a mixing bowl huge enough to hold two boxes of cereal. An opened book is on the table next to the bowl.

"Man, he can put it away, can't he?" Cal says loud enough for Zachary to turn around and yank back the curtain. I wiggle, trying to free Cal's grasp around my ankles, but instead Cal's grip tightens and together we fall to the asphalt.

"What are you looking at, perverts?" Zachary yells. And even though the window is closed, his words pierce through the glass and pound our ears. He slides open the window. "If you Peeping Toms don't get out of here, I'll call the cops."

Cal and I race to our bikes, accidentally grabbing each other's, not bothering to switch until we're safe at home.

Chapter Five

The day after Zachary Beaver catches Cal and me peeking into his trailer, we head over to the library to find out if he really is the fattest boy in the world. When I was little, Mom would take me there each week for Miss Myrtie Mae's story time, but I haven't stepped inside the library in ages. Neither has Cal.

We look through the door window. Miss Myrtie Mae sits behind an oak desk, peering over her wire-framed glasses, studying some black-and-white photos. She does a double take when we enter. "Haven't seen you boys in here in a decade. Anything I can help you with?"

"No, ma'am," we answer together, heading toward the other side of the room.

Dust particles spin under the overhead lights, and the moldy smell of old books fills the air. Cal and I wander around, our eyes scanning the shelves.

Treasure Island, the Hardy Boys Mysteries, and *Old Yeller* remind me of nights when Mom read to me before bedtime.

"It wouldn't be over here," I whisper. "This is fiction."

"Did you say something?" Miss Myrtie Mae asks.

I shake my head. "Oh, no, ma'am. I was talking to Cal."

She nods and looks down at the pictures.

I glance across the room. Letters cut from construction paper spell *Nonfiction* above a bookcase. The shelves contain books about rattlesnakes, space, and gemstones. There are also books about the American Revolutionary War and biographies on a few presidents. But there isn't a copy of the *Guinness Book of World Records.*

"It's not here," Cal says.

"Are you looking for this?" Miss Myrtie Mae asks, holding up a blue hardback book.

Cal steps up to her desk, and I follow. Miss Myrtie Mae holds out the *Guinness Book of World Records.* "Thanks!" Cal hollers.

"You're welcome," she says, returning to her photos. I nudge closer and notice her pictures of Zachary Beaver's trailer and of people waiting in line to see him.

I look over Cal's shoulder as he thumbs through the book.

"Pages fifteen and sixteen," says Miss Myrtie Mae, not even glancing up.

Cal turns to page fifteen and finds the subtitle "Heaviest Man."

I stare at Miss Myrtie Mae, puzzled. *How did she know?*

Her gray eyebrows hike above her glasses. "You think you're the first person who came sniffing around about that boy? I've seen more people in this library the last couple of days than I've seen all year."

"Oh," I say, embarrassed to be lumped in with the same group of nosy people.

"He's not in there," she states.

We keep reading, looking at the pictures, searching for anything about Zachary.

Miss Myrtie Mae shrugs. "Suit yourself."

She's right. The book lists that the fattest man now living is reported to weigh 739 pounds. It also shows a picture of the heaviest man of all time wearing a pair of gigantic overalls. The book says that at the time his picture was taken, he weighed seven hundred pounds. He died when he was thirty-two years old and was buried in a piano case. I wonder if that's Zachary Beaver's destiny.

"He's a lot bigger than Zachary Beaver," Cal says.

"Give him time," I say.

Cal scratches his head. "But if Zachary weighs 643 pounds, he should be near that size. He must be lying."

Miss Myrtie Mae's eyes narrow to staples. "What difference should it make? If he wants to call himself the fattest boy in the world, what harm is it doing to you?"

Cal and I don't answer. We hand back the book, thank her, and leave, ending our once-in-a-decade visit to the Antler Public Library.

⌒

For the first time in a year Dad treats me to lunch at the Bowl-a-Rama Cafe. Dad would just as soon eat paper as Ferris's greasy food. He believes you are what you eat. But he's in a good mood because "Super Mex" Lee Trevino won the British Open this weekend. When Trevino came on the pro golf circuit a few years ago, he was considered the underdog—a poor Mexican American guy from El Paso. Dad always roots for the underdogs. It doesn't matter where they're from. He cheered for the Boston Red Sox long before they won the American League pennant, in '67.

Before we enter the Bowl-a-Rama, I glance across the street. The trailer is still parked in the Dairy Maid parking lot and Paulie Rankin's car is still missing.

"Hey, Toby!" I hear Cal's voice, but I don't see him. I look up, shading my eyes from the sun. Cal is perched on the roof of the Bowl-a-Rama, our getaway spot.

"Thought you'd be working."

"Dad gave me the day off because Kate went to take her driving test and Billy had to go to work early."

"Come join us for lunch, Cal," Dad says. "I'm treating."

Never one to turn down a free meal, Cal climbs down the metal ladder hooked on the side of the building.

"Does Ferris know you're up there?" Dad asks.

"He doesn't care," Cal says. "We do it all the time."

Dad examines me, eyebrows raised. "Oh?"

Cal smacks my back.

"Ow!"

"Paulie's car is still gone."

"I know, Cal. I've got eyes too."

As soon as we step inside the cafe, I breathe in the spicy smells. Ferris's chalkboard hangs near the kitchen window behind the counter. *Today's Special: Honey Fried Chicken, Corn Fritters, and Mustard Greens.* Beneath the menu is the daily Bible verse. *"It is an honor for a man to cease from strife: but every fool will be meddling." Proverbs 20:3.* Mom says some people wear their religion on their sleeves. Ferris posts his on the chalkboard.

Southern gospel music plays from the jukebox, but the sound of bowling balls hitting pins in the next room can still be heard. From the kitchen window, Ima Jean stares at us through her steamed-up cat-eyed glasses. With the back of her hand, she wipes them in a circular motion.

Ferris does a double take when he sees Dad. "How ya doing, Otto? Haven't seen you in a long time."

Dad nods toward Ferris. "Doing fine. Yourself?"

Ferris strokes his beard stubble. "Couldn't be better. Sure do miss your woman, though."

Dad glances at the Good Luck, Opalina! sign hanging over the counter. His temples pulse, and he averts his eyes to the floor. The ice machine moans, dropping a load of ice. We walk to a corner table, and Ferris limps our way with a menu. His watermelon belly hangs over his belt, and a patch of hairy skin peeks through a gap between two buttons.

Soon the regular lunch crowd begins to pour inside the cafe—the Shriners in their tall hats and decorated vests, the farmers with their sons, and Earline, the only real estate lady in Antler. In fact, that's what it says on her Volkswagen—Earline Carter, the Real Estate Lady. As if in a town our size, we wouldn't know who she was. If she mashed down her black bee-hive hairdo, she would probably only be four feet tall. Today, despite all the hairpins and spray, her beehive is leaning like the Tower of Pisa. "Hello, Otto. How's Opalina?"

"Fine."

"I guess this is her shot at the big time, isn't it? She's a brave woman, going all the way to Nashville. Alone at that. You're mighty brave to let her." She raises her eyebrows, waiting.

A hush falls over the cafe, but Dad doesn't say anything. The only sound comes from the jukebox, where another record drops in place. Elvis begins singing "The Old Rugged Cross." Earline squirms and brushes imaginary lint off her sleeve.

Miss Myrtie Mae comes in the cafe with the Judge. He's been retired for years, but everyone still greets him that way. Like Miss Myrtie Mae, he's long and skinny, but a good ten years older than her. His thick white hair is combed back with no part and his cheeks sink into his face, forming valleys below his high cheekbones.

Miss Myrtie Mae selects the table in front of us. "Sit here, Brother." As always she wears her straw hat and pointy shoes.

The Judge settles in the chair and starts tinkering

with his gold pocket watch. Miss Myrtie Mae nods at Dad. "Otto," she says, "Brother and I would sure appreciate it if Toby would mow our yard the rest of the summer. We'd pay him a fair price."

I wonder why she doesn't ask me, when I'm sitting right here.

Dad looks at me, eyebrows raised. "Toby?"

"Yes, ma'am. I'll be happy to mow it." There are worse things to do than mowing Miss Myrtie Mae's lawn—like taking care of worms. Besides, I could use the money.

Cal's face turns red as his hair. He's tapping a straw against his glass, and his tongue makes a lump in his cheek. It dawns on me that Billy mowed Miss Myrtie Mae's yard the last two summers and Wayne did it before that. I guess Cal thought he'd be the natural choice.

"Fridays be okay?" she asks.

"Yes, ma'am."

"Order out!" hollers Ima Jean through the window. Ferris heads over to pick up the plates.

Outside, I see Wylie Womack park his golf cart across the square in the shade of the giant elm, the same place he's parked every summer day I can remember. His long salt-and-pepper hair swings in front of his face as he struggles to get out of the cart, pop open his wheelchair, and settle in. As if Wylie Womack doesn't have enough problems with his crooked body, he also has emphysema. But Wylie doesn't let that slow him down. His motorized chair moves easily along the side of his cart.

I smell fresh coffee and look around, expecting to see Mom pouring some in Earline's cup. For a little person Mom sure leaves a big hole. If she wins the contest and gets a record deal, I guess Dad and I will have to blow this town and move to Nashville. Dad will rent the longest U-Haul trailer and pack up his worms, and we'll split down the road. Funny thing is, every time I try to picture Dad and me going to Nashville, Dad comes out like a blur in an overexposed photo.

Even though I know the menu by heart, I read the words over and over, trying not to think about Zachary Beaver over at the trailer or where Paulie Rankin went.

Ferris returns to take our order, and Cal asks, "Hey, any word on that freak show guy?"

"Haven't seen hide nor hair of him."

"Strangest fella," Earline says, overhearing our conversation.

"Where do you think he went?" I ask.

"Tobias," Dad says, his mind-your-own-business tone attached. He's studying the menu and doesn't even look up when he says my name.

"Don't know," Ferris says. "It's got the best of me."

Earline looks up. "Whatever it is, it must be no good." She scoots her chair away from the table, causing it to screech. "I suspect the sheriff will be looking into it."

Miss Myrtie Mae sets down a saltine cracker and scowls at Earline. "A stranger can't spend five minutes in Antler without everybody suspecting he's a serial killer. Can they, Brother?"

The Judge doesn't answer. He stares in my direction; his dark beady eyes burn a hole right through me.

"Well," Earline says, walking out the door, "decent people don't leave a child unattended for days on end." She turns and looks at Miss Myrtie Mae. "Do they?"

Ignoring Earline, Miss Myrtie Mae picks up her cracker and takes a bite. Her mouth chews in exaggerated circles.

Ferris chuckles. "If Opalina had been here, she would make up a song about it. Probably something like 'The Ballad of Zachary Beaver.' "

Everyone laughs but Dad. He glances up from his menu. "I'll take a bowl of tomato soup."

Before going home, we buy a snow cone from Wylie. Wylie hasn't spoken in years, I guess on account of the emphysema. His cart is built low so that he can reach the ice machine and syrup bottles. Every Thursday the ice man delivers ice to the Bowl-a-Rama Cafe. Ferris lets Wylie keep the ice in his huge freezer since Wylie rents a room at the Sunset Motel and doesn't have a place to store it.

The colored bottles glisten in the sun. Grape, lemon, orange, watermelon, strawberry, bubble gum. They all look tempting, but as always, Cal and I order Bahama Mamas. While we suck the sweet red juice through our straws, I can't help thinking about Wayne. Cal must be too because before taking his first bite, he says, "Got a letter from Wayne today."

"How is your brother, Cal?" Dad asks.

"Fine. He sure misses home."

"I'll bet he does. Be good to have him back." A few years ago, Wayne helped Dad build the shelter for his worms in our backyard. Dad told him more than anyone would ever care to know about Tennessee brown nose fishing worms. I'm sure Wayne would have preferred talking about baseball or girls or anything besides worms. But Wayne would smile, nod, and ask Dad questions like he was really interested.

While Dad stops into the insurance office across the square, Cal and I eat our snow cones.

"Hey, watch this," Cal says, taking off for the trailer.

"Get back here!" My heart pounds in my ears.

Wylie watches us, a blank expression on his face. I glance toward the insurance company. Dad's back side is to the trailer door.

Cal races up to the trailer, sets his half-eaten snow cone on the top step, knocks on the door, and runs back toward me.

"Cal, are you crazy?"

"Maybe he's thirsty."

We watch. Nothing happens. Even the wind is calm, as if it too is waiting. The cup sits on the top step, the red straw poking out of the snow cone.

Dad returns. "Ready, boys?"

We get into the truck and head home. But as we drive away, Wylie points in the direction of the trailer. We look and see a pale hand extend out the trailer door and grab the cup. Cal and I exchange glances but don't say a word.

It only takes a minute to reach home. Next door, Kate sits in the driver's seat of the station wagon, parked in front of their mailbox. She rolls down the window and holds up a small square piece of paper. "I got it! I got it!"

Dad thrusts his fist in the air. "That's great!"

I send her the thumbs-up sign, and even Cal calls out, "All right! Let's go for a ride."

Smiling, she waves, rolls up the window, and puts

the car in reverse. And she's still smiling and waving as she hits the mailbox and it crashes on the asphalt.

While Dad rushes over to her, Cal shrugs and shakes his head. "Now I know what we can do with all those smashed-up garbage cans."

"What?" I ask.

"Make helmets for everybody in town. We're going to need them when Kate gets on the road."

Chapter Six

We can see all of Antler from the flat roof of the Bowl-a-Rama. We see the cotton fields and the cattle ranches stretched out beyond the town limits. We see hundreds of cars and trucks whizzing down the highway on their way to anywhere but here. And sky. We see lots and lots of sky. But today Cal and I have our eyes glued on one item—the grocery sack we just left on Zachary Beaver's trailer step. We lie bellies down on the roof and wait.

It's been three days since Paulie Rankin left, and we figure a big guy like Zachary must be running out of food. I brought tomatoes, butter beans, and onions from Dad's garden. Cal brought Twinkies, potato chips, and hot dogs.

Today I was the one who went to Zachary's door. I set down the sack, knocked, then ran across the street and climbed the Bowl-a-Rama ladder to the roof.

We watch the trailer door, but now we also watch anybody who passes or drives by. It amounts to Earline driving her Volkswagen to the courthouse, Malcolm and Mason going inside the Dairy Maid, and Miss Myrtie Mae heading over to the library, wearing her wide-brim straw hat.

"To protect her virgin skin," I say in my high-pitch imitation of Miss Myrtie Mae.

Cal hoots. "That ain't the only thing virgin about her." Cal's hand covers his heart. "Miss Myrtie Mae has a tragic past."

"How's that?" I ask.

"The fellas at the gin said when Miss Myrtie Mae was younger she was engaged to a lawyer from Wichita Falls. All her sisters had married and moved away. She and the Judge were left. Two nights before the wedding the Judge pretended to be on his deathbed. She postponed the wedding, but the lawyer broke up with her because he said she was already married."

"What did he mean by that?"

"He meant the Judge. The fellas at the gin say she was so dedicated to him, she would never have room for a real husband. After the lawyer broke up with her, the Judge made a remarkable recovery. Miss Myrtie Mae's only chance at love, and it was gone." Cal pretends to play a violin.

I don't like thinking of love and Miss Myrtie Mae in the same sentence. Especially since I seem to be as unlucky at it as she is. "Heard from Wayne?" I ask.

Cal sits up. "Almost forgot. I got another letter." He digs into his shorts pocket and reads it aloud.

Dear Cal,

Hope this letter finds you having a great week and that you are having the best summer ever. Have you had the Ladybug Waltz yet?

Our food supply has been low this week, so we haven't had as much to eat lately. Those chocolate bars Mom sent have sure come in handy. It's not that bad, though. Starting tomorrow, we'll have liberty for two days in Saigon, and I'm going to order the biggest meal I can find. After that, we'll be heading out, and I should see a lot more action. Remember when you, Billy, and me played war in the backyard? I guess I'll get to see it for real now. Don't worry about me. I've had a lot of practice throwing water balloons.

How is Mom? I'll bet her roses are really pretty this time of year. And I guess Dad is working as hard as always. Now, there's something I don't miss—hoeing that Johnson grass during the blistering heat.

Cal, I'd love to hear from you sometime. I guess you're like I was at your age, trying to crowd a lot of fun into every minute of summer before you have to go back to school. You and Toby have a blast on me, okay?

> *Your brother,*
> *Wayne*

"Did you write him back?" I ask.

Cal scratches the back of his neck. "Not yet."

I glance away. "You ought to write him."

"Hey, man, give me a break. I got the letter today. Besides, Kate writes him every day. I don't know what she has to write about. She's the most boring ugly person alive."

Time drags on. Our sweat attracts the flies from the Dumpster below, and our shirts stick to our backs. Out of nowhere Cal says, "Maybe Zachary is dead."

"Jeez, Cal!"

"Well, he hasn't answered the door."

"Maybe we should knock again."

But before we take off, the curtain in the trailer parts an inch.

We don't stir. We don't speak. We don't even breathe.

A moment later the door opens a crack, and though we can't see anything, we know Zachary Beaver is peeking through. The door swings open, and now we see all of Zachary as he bends down and lifts the grocery sack. He is huge. Bare chested. His gut tumbles out over his pants. His arms are rolls of dough, and his puffy bare feet peek out of his baggy pants legs. He struggles to stand, gripping the doorway to balance. And when he does stand, we see he has breasts like a woman. Even with the noise of the Bowl-a-Rama's air-conditioning unit, we hear him take a big breath before slamming the door.

"Whoa!" Cal says. "That's a whole lot of person. He could wear a bigger bra than flat-chested Kate."

I wonder what it would be like to be that fat. Once when I was nine or ten, Mom heard that a cold front might blow through the Panhandle. It was fifty degrees outside, but she made me wear a bulky sweater and my heavy winter coat. The cold front never arrived, and I felt like an enormous snowman, sweating under all those layers. I wonder if that's how Zachary feels every minute.

Mission is accomplished with the food delivered, and so we decide to go home.

"Go on without me," I tell Cal. "Dad asked me to stop at the Wag-a-Bag for milk and bread."

He starts for the ladder, jumps from the second step, and hops on his bike. At the bottom of the ladder, I notice he's dropped Wayne's letter. Since Cal is way down the road past the square, I tuck the letter into my pocket. I'll give it back to him later. But right now, for this short time, the letter is mine.

Chapter Seven

Four days have passed since Paulie Rankin left town. Today Cal and I place another sack of groceries on Zachary Beaver's steps. We've been here an hour, and he still hasn't opened the door. We wait and wait. I wonder if we wait to make sure he picks up the groceries or to get another glimpse of him.

At least today we came prepared, armed with a Sugar Daddy apiece, jawbreakers, and M&M's. Our teeth sticky from the caramel, we talk about Paulie Rankin. We even make up his history—where he was born and how he ended up as a sideshow owner. First we have Paulie figured out as a bank robber who uses Zachary Beaver to distract the law. Then we have him dodging a loan shark. Finally we decide he kidnapped Zachary and is hiding out from an orthodontist because of an unpaid bill.

While we wait, Malcolm's little brother, Mason, and four other chubby third graders show up with sticks in their hands. Unlike Malcolm, Mason is tough and the leader of his bully pack. Each kid takes a side of the trailer and starts hitting it with sticks. Over their pounding, Mason yells, "Hey, fat boy! Show your face!"

Something boils inside me. I remember when kids like them beat up on me just because they could. I wouldn't snitch, and since Dad was against it, I wouldn't fight back either. But today is different. Today we're soldiers, fighting for Zachary.

Thinking fast, Cal and I climb down the ladder and scoop up rocks from Ferris's rock pile out back. They're not big rocks, but from the roof they could sting the little brats' arms, backs, and behinds. Using our shirts as baskets, we carry the rocks to the roof.

Cal and I stand next to each other, our legs apart like camera tripods, our arms set in pitching positions. "Ready."

"Aim." I focus on Mason's butt.

"Fire." My rock sails through the air and hits a perfect target.

Mason's hands fly to his porky bottom. "Ow!" He looks up at the roof, shading his eyes with one hand.

When Cal hits Simon Davis's leg, Simon takes off crying, his hand pressed against his thigh. Cal trots in place. "And this little piggy went wee, wee, wee, all the way home!"

I throw again, this time aiming at James Rutherford's arm. I miss. Then I hear it. Glass breaking. The window shatters, and the boys scatter in different directions.

"Run!" yells Cal, and we do, leaving our bikes next to the ladder.

It's Thursday, and I wake up to the radio DJ yelling, "One more day until TGIF!"

Two things weigh heavy on my mind—Zachary's broken window and Mom's big night tonight. Nashville time is one hour ahead of us, but she's probably sleeping in. I picture her lying in a dark hotel room, eye mask covering her eyes, Dad's worn-out socks on her hands to lock in her Avon hand cream, and empty orange juice cans she uses for rollers crowded on her head. It's the best way, she says, to get big hair. I say it's the best way to get a big headache.

Since summer nights are usually cool in Antler, we sleep with the windows open and leave them that way until noon. But this morning the air conditioner is already running at full speed, so I get up and shut the window. Just as I'm about to flick the lock, I see the sheriff's car pull up in front. Sheriff Levi gets out and walks toward our house. Duke hangs his head out the window, his tongue draping from his mouth.

My stomach plunges. Zachary Beaver must have squealed. Maybe he saw us running away. Or it might have been nosy Earline, looking out her real estate office window. She has a full view of the trailer from her desk. I thought real estate agents answered the phone and showed homes to people, but Earline seems to do anything but that. Once I walked by her office window and found Earline with her feet propped up on the desk, painting her toenails. Cotton balls stuck between each toe.

From the living room Dad calls, "Toby!"

I feel sick. I yank on a pair of shorts and run downstairs. Sheriff Levi's arms are folded across his chest, and except for his usual eye twitch, his face looks blank. He pulls off his hat and rakes his fingers through his wavy hair.

I check out Dad's face, but it doesn't tell me anything except he hasn't shaved yet. "Toby, Sheriff Levi has something to ask you."

He's heard. Maybe I should confess. But Cal would get in trouble, and I'm not a snitch like Malcolm.

Sheriff Levi clears his throat, and his right eye twitches like crazy. "Toby, I have a favor to ask of you."

My stomach feels like a glob of lava in a Lava lamp, slowly floating up toward my throat.

"Toby, reckon you and Cal could accompany me to that sideshow trailer?"

I don't know what to say. My knees shake, and the sheriff's eye twitches.

"Toby," Dad says, "the sheriff is asking you something."

"Sir?"

"I need to find out what those fellas' plans are, and since he's just a kid, I don't want to scare him or anything. Seeing a sheriff at your door can be intimidating. You know what I mean?"

He continues explaining. "Since you boys are about his age, maybe he'd relax a bit, open up and tell me the whereabouts of that other guy. The Dairy Maid has been mighty patient with them parked out front. Before he left, that sideshow fella paid them cash for the water and electricity hookup, but he said it would only be for a few days.

"Yesterday Ferris got an envelope in the mail from that guy with money for some meals for that boy. It had a San Francisco postmark, but no return address. Now the folks at the Dairy Maid want to know what's going on. Don't blame them one bit. And, well, it's my job to make sure strangers have a good reason for sticking around Antler."

Sheriff Levi doesn't mention the broken window. Bringing him straight to Zachary Beaver's door would be like asking me to pick out the electric chair for my own execution. Zachary probably assumes we broke it since he caught us peeking in it a few days ago.

"Tobias," Dad says, raising his eyebrow, "the sheriff is waiting for your answer."

I have no choice. "Yes, sir. Yes, sir, I'll be ready in a second."

Duke rides shotgun in the front while Cal and I ride in the backseat of the sheriff's car. I hold a sack of bell peppers and green onions Dad packed for me to give to Zachary. Cal acts like we're going on a field trip to Disneyland. I feel like I'm attending a funeral—mine. As we pull up in front of the trailer, I check out our bikes still leaning against the side of the Bowl-a-Rama.

Sheriff Levi parks his car and Cal bounces out. I take my time. As we walk up to the trailer, the sheriff looks toward the broken window, which is now covered with Wag-a-Bag grocery sacks. He tilts up his hat. "Wonder how that happened?"

After the sheriff knocks on Zachary's door, we wait

for Zachary to answer. When he doesn't, I'm thinking, Good, maybe we can leave. But Sheriff Levi knocks again and hollers, "Mr. Beaver, Sheriff Levi Fetterman here. I need a minute of your time, please."

The door slowly creaks open a few inches and Zachary peeks through with one eye. He huffs, beads of sweat rolling down his face like he ran the fifty-yard dash.

The sheriff clears his throat. "Mr. Beaver, sorry if I woke you, but I need to ask you a few questions. I brought along a couple of my young friends. This is Toby and Cal."

Zachary's eye narrows, and I know he remembers. I hold my breath, waiting for his finger to point our way. But he only nods and says, "We've met."

"Can we come in?" asks Sheriff Levi.

Zachary swings open the trailer door and we step inside. The smell of lemon Pledge makes me think back to the first day Zachary arrived. He's wearing a long red nightshirt like I saw in *The Night Before Christmas*. The ball of Zachary's right foot is wrapped loosely with gauze. Malcolm wears a size twelve, and Zachary's feet look a lot bigger. He wobbles across the room, the floor creaking with each step, and flops on the love seat, his bottom covering both cushions. He doesn't ask us to sit down, but there's no place to sit anyway. The Plexiglas panels rest next to the wall, folded like an Oriental screen. I see the fabric panel hanging at the other end of the trailer and wonder if the bathroom is behind it.

Sheriff Levi leans against an empty space on the wall. Cal looks around, his eyes casing out the place, and I can see his fingers itching to touch something. I take deep breaths through my nose and try to look relaxed. In one hand I hold the sack of vegetables, but I don't know what to do with my other hand. Finally I let it hang at my side.

Sheriff Levi glances around. "Nice little place you have here. You got about everything you need."

"It'll do," says Zachary.

The sheriff walks over to the window with the bags taped over it. "Looks like you have a problem with that window, though. Know anything about that?"

I hold my breath, concentrate on the floor, and prepare for the ax to fall.

Zachary stares at us, yawns, and locks his hands behind his head. "I guess some kids did it."

"Well, I'll drop by later with somebody who can fix that for you."

My heartbeat slows and my breathing returns to a regular pace now that I know Zachary doesn't have a clue it was us.

"Toby and Cal should be about your age," Sheriff Levi says. "How old are you fellas?"

"Thirteen," we say together.

"I'm fifteen," says Zachary, and the way he says it sounds like he thinks fifteen is as old as thirty.

"That a fact?" says the sheriff.

Zachary just stares.

Sheriff Levi folds his arms and clears his throat. "Mr. Beaver, you don't sound like a Texan."

"I'm from New York. New York City. Ever heard of it?"

Sheriff Levi grins. "Kind of a jokester, aren't you?" He looks down at Zachary's foot, and his smile drops into a frown. "What happened to your foot?"

Zachary covers his injured foot with his left one. "It's okay. I just stepped on a piece of glass."

The sheriff kneels in front of Zachary like a shoe salesman. "You better let me take a look at that."

"It's okay," Zachary snaps.

Sheriff Levi stands and steps back. "All right, but I'm sure the doctor at the clinic would be glad to take a look at it."

Zachary glares.

Sheriff Levi clears his throat. "Where is that other fella from? The young man you're traveling with?"

"Paulie? He's from Jersey."

"Is that where he is now?"

"No."

"Where is he, son?"

"He's looking for another act to add to our show, but I don't know where he is."

Zachary frowns at Cal, who is lifting the lid off the gold box. "Put it down. My mom gave that to me."

Cal lifts a black book out of the box. "It's just a Bible."

"It's not *just* a Bible. My mom gave it to me when I got baptized."

Cal flips to the front pages.

"Cal, put the boy's Bible down," Sheriff Levi says in a gentle tone. Cal slaps the Bible shut and returns it to the box.

I'm wondering why Levi Fetterman ever became sheriff. He's too soft, and I can tell he hates asking these questions by the way his eye twitches and he keeps clearing his throat.

"Where are your parents?" Sheriff Levi asks.

"Rosemont Cemetery."

"How's that?"

"Dead."

Sheriff Levi clears his throat, and his eye looks like it's going to take off. "Sorry about that, son. Life can be tough."

"I'm not your son," Zachary says.

The sheriff swallows. "Well, of course not. Sorry. Didn't mean to offend you. Who is your legal guardian?"

"Paulie Rankin's my guardian."

Sheriff Levi grimaces, and his voice becomes firm. "I see. Well, I hate to break this to you, Mr. Beaver, but if Mr. Rankin doesn't return in a week, I'm going to have to take some sort of action. I really should be doing it now. This isn't a campground, and the court would view you as a minor who has been left unsupervised and abandoned."

"Paulie will be back. He always comes back."

"How do you know?" the sheriff asks.

"I'm his bread and butter."

Sheriff Levi looks at Zachary with pity, and I wonder if he's thinking about taking him home like one of his adopted dogs. "How is your food supply?"

"Fine. As you can see, I'm not starving."

Sheriff Levi turns to leave. "Well, you fellas stay and get acquainted. Maybe you could invite Zachary to pal around with you." I try to picture Zachary riding a bike or climbing on top of the Bowl-a-Rama, but the bike tires flatten and the ladder steps to the roof break.

The sheriff's hand rests on the doorknob. "Mr.

Beaver, you enjoy your stay in Antler. But I hope your friend returns by the end of next week. I truly hope he does. And one more thing, you can expect a visit from the doctor about that foot."

The sheriff leaves, and Zachary smirks at the closed door. "Oooh, he's got me shaking in my boots."

I want to tell him how lucky he is that the sheriff hasn't hauled his butt off to New York City. Instead I hold out the sack of bell peppers and green onions to Zachary. "I brought you some vegetables. They're from my dad's garden."

"The refrigerator is behind you," Zachary says. In Antler it's considered rude to order people around and not even say thank you for a gift, but I remember his parents are dead. If I were an orphan, I probably wouldn't have any manners.

I expect an empty refrigerator, but it's stocked with food. Among the eggs, cheese, and milk is a Bowl-a-Rama barbecue plate and a Chicken Delight casserole covered in plastic wrapping. Ferris must have already visited Zachary, and there is only one person in Antler who makes Chicken Delight casserole—Miss Myrtie Mae Pruitt. Just when I think there isn't anything I don't know about boring Antler, something happens and takes me by surprise.

Zachary sneezes so loud, it sounds like the roof could cave in. "It sure gets dusty here quick," he says.

"It's the wind," I explain. "It blows all the time."

Zachary points to the light fixture. "Could you dust that? I hurt my back picking up the glass."

"No sweat," Cal says since he's the only one who can reach it. A second later Zachary has me dusting the end table. He's bossy and grumpy, and if I didn't give it any thought earlier, I've decided I don't much like Zachary Beaver. But the dusting is the least I can do, considering I broke the window.

Cal dusts the lower bookshelf while trying to take a peek at the albums. "I can reach *that*," Zachary snaps.

With a shrug, Cal leaves the cloth on the shelf. "Hey, this is neat." He grabs a book titled *Sideshows*.

"That's Paulie's," Zachary growls. "Put it back."

Slowly Cal returns the book to the shelf. "Are you in there?"

"Nope."

"Who's in there?"

"A bunch of old acts. Most of the people are dead or retired. But one day I'll be in a book."

"How's that?" I ask, thinking about what Cal and I discovered at the library.

"One day Paulie and I will both be in a book

because we're going to have the biggest sideshow business ever."

I force a laugh. "You mean the smallest. You're only one act."

"Not for long," Zachary says. Maybe Paulie Rankin is really out drumming up more business. Maybe he's looking for a two-headed person or a turtle man.

"Who usually does the cleaning for you?" I ask.

"Paulie. What do you cowboys do around here for fun?"

"We're not cowboys," I snap, wondering why I'm helping this guy who thinks he's such a big shot.

"Isn't this Texas, where the buffalos roam and the deer and the antelope play?"

I throw down the dust rag. "Not everybody in Texas has a ranch."

"What do your parents do, then?"

Cal flops on the floor. "My dad grows cotton. Toby's dad is the postmaster, but he also raises worms."

My ears burn.

Zachary laughs. "Worms?"

"Yeah, worms," I say. "It's not like he travels around in a trailer and charges people to look at him or anything."

I expect him to snap back, but he rubs his chin. "And what do people do with *worms*?"

My mouth opens, and I repeat all the things Dad has ever bored me with about worms. "Worms are being used in Florida to help break down landfills, and their soil makes some of the richest fertilizer on the earth. Cal's mom uses it on her roses, and she grows some of the best in Antl—in Texas. And—"

"Mostly people use them for fishing," says Cal. I want to bust his lip. I know I'm trying to make my dad sound as important as the United States president.

"Some French people eat worms," Zachary says.

"I know that," I say, but really I've never heard of anything more ridiculous.

"You like to shoot cans?" Cal asks.

"Shoot cans? Is that what you do around here for fun?"

"Well, what do *you* do for fun, besides watching TV and reading?" I ask him.

Zachary smirks. "Nothing around here. But I've done plenty."

"Like what?" I ask, and the way he meets my gaze, he knows I'm challenging him.

"Like ride the elevator to the top of the Eiffel Tower and cross the London Bridge and look out from the top of Seattle's Space Needle."

When we leave, Zachary adds, "Oh, don't forget your bikes. You left them by the Bowl-a-Rama yesterday."

Outside the trailer, I ask Cal why Zachary didn't squeal on us.

"Maybe he has a few secrets of his own."

"What do you mean?" I ask.

"Well, for one thing—Paulie Rankin. I think Zachary knows where he's at. And we already know he's probably not the fattest boy in the world. And then there's that Bible. He said his mom gave it to him when he was baptized."

"So?"

"Iola Beaver, I guess that's his mom, gave him the Bible. Her name is in there, but the baptism information is blank. If you're given a Bible when you're baptized, wouldn't that be the first blank you filled in? It doesn't make sense."

And for once, Cal does.

Chapter Eight

"She didn't win." Dad says the words at dinner like he's asking me to pass the salt.

Although I feel a twinge of disappointment for Mom because I know how much she wanted to win, I'm relieved. "Then she'll be coming home tomorrow?"

Dad stirs his peas into the mashed potatoes on his plate. He's getting pretty good at cooking vegetables, but his mashed potatoes are lumpy. And of course, there's no gravy.

"She'll be staying on awhile."

"What do you mean? If she lost, why is she staying?"

"She got runner-up, and apparently some hotshot manager in the audience thinks he can get her a record deal."

Suddenly nothing on my plate looks good. "How long will that take?"

Dad finally looks at me. "Those kind of things can take a long time, Toby."

"How long?"

He looks me square in the eyes. "Sometimes they never happen."

"Well, Mom wouldn't stay forever. How long will she stay?" I'm almost yelling.

"Toby, I'm not the person to answer that question. I'll give you her phone number and you can ask her yourself."

"Yeah. Give me the number. I'll call her."

Dad shakes his head, gets up, and goes into the kitchen. The way he walks with his jaw set and shoulders stiff reminds me of something I had forgotten or blocked out. *The fight*. Their last fight. It was in this room. At this table. Dad got up and stomped away, angry, while Mom continued to yell at the wall. Shutting my eyes tight, I try to erase that memory, but it plays over and over in my mind. And the strangest thing is I don't even remember what the argument was about.

Dad stands in front of me, a piece of paper in his hand.

I take it, push my chair away from the table, and run up the stairs. I grab the hall phone with the long extension, take it into my room, and stretch out on my bed. I start to dial the number, then stop. I don't need to talk to Mom. She won't stay away long. She wouldn't. After all, she didn't take her old guitar and pearl necklace. She would have taken them for sure if she wasn't coming back.

And if Mom does get a record deal, she'll send for me in a heartbeat. We'll travel around the country in her big bus that says Opalina Wilson and the Delta Boys or whatever her backup group is. I'll count her money for her. I'll be her manager. I'll be the youngest manager in the history of country music. Probably in the history of any kind of music. The Delta Boys will call me Tex. I close my eyes and watch the tail end of that big bus ride down Interstate 40 to towns where people crowd into concert arenas to hear Mom. My breaths even out with each billboard we pass.

When I wake up, the clock on my nightstand reads ten minutes past ten, and for a minute I don't know if it's the same night or the next day. Outside my window, stars twinkle in a dark sky. I've been asleep for three hours. The pants I wore yesterday are slung across my chair, and Cal's letter from Wayne is poking out of the back pocket. I forgot to return it to Cal today, but he never mentioned losing it. Goofy Cal probably doesn't even know he dropped it yet.

I get up, pull out the letter, and read it again and again. Then I tear a piece of paper from last year's math notebook and write a letter to Wayne. I tell him all the things Cal and I are doing. I tell him about Kate getting her driver's license, his mom's roses, and Zachary Beaver coming to town. I tell him that the ladybugs haven't arrived yet and that we ate Bahama Mama snow cones at Wylie Womack's stand and thought of him. I tell him all these things and more. And then I sign—*Sincerely, your brother, Cal*.

A few minutes pass, and I hear Dad snoring down the hall. Holding my shoes, I walk down the stairs and try to keep the steps from creaking. Outside, I get on my bike and ride to the mailbox in front of the post office before heading to the lake. It's cool, and the breeze feels good against my face. I open my mouth, wishing I could swallow enough air to lift me like a hot-air balloon and carry me away from this stinking town.

At the lake I jump off my bike, run up to the water, and lie sprawled flat on the grass, looking up at the millions of stars and the full moon. The moon reminds me of times when I was five or six and couldn't fall asleep. Mom would slip into my bed next to me and shine the flashlight on the dark ceiling.

"See the moon," she'd say, pointing to the perfect round light. "Let's make it dance." She'd move the flashlight, causing our moon to trot or waltz back and forth across the ceiling. We'd laugh, and she'd make that moon dance until my eyes got so drowsy, I fell asleep. Of course, that was kid stuff. These days I lull myself to sleep thinking of Scarlett swinging back and forth on her porch swing.

Music softly plays, and I figure it's from some house far away, but the sound gets closer. James Taylor is singing "You've Got a Friend."

"Are you okay?" Scarlett stands above me, holding a transistor radio. I look at her red toenails and wonder if she puts cotton balls between each one before painting them.

Most guys would jump up, but I lie there like a dork and squeak, "Yeah, I'm fine." I don't know what it is about this girl that makes my voice go up two octaves.

"Are you sure?" From the ground, I have an incredible view of her long legs wearing a pair of short white cutoffs. Now is a good time to get up, but I stay there, stretched out on the ground like some corpse. "Yeah, kind of tired. Rough day at the office." My ears are on fire. All the words in Webster's dictionary and I choose those.

Finally I sit up. "Do you come here often?" I ask. Each second I approach dork eternity. But she doesn't seem to notice.

"Not that often. Only when I break up with a guy."

"You broke up with Juan?" I try not to sound too excited, but my words come out squeaky. If I stay calm, I'll have this voice thing under control. Though it's hard to stay calm.

"Yeah, looks that way." Her voice quivers, and she chews on a long strand of hair. She's just inches from me. I want to reach for her, pull her toward me, and tell her it will be all right. I want to smooth her hair, massage her neck, kiss her toes. Instead I wrap my arms around my knees.

"Why'd you break up?"

"He stood me up. He said he'd go with me to my great-grandfather's birthday in Amarillo. We gave him a big fancy party for turning eighty."

"Man, that's old."

Scarlett sits next to me. A shiver runs through my body. "For two months Juan kept saying he was going. Then at the last minute, he backed out. He didn't even give me a good reason."

"What a jerk," I say in a deep voice.

"Do you have a cold?" she asks.

I skip a rock across the water, thankful that it's dark because my face feels red.

I'm feeling guilty for all the things I'm thinking about, but I know I would be in heaven just holding Scarlett Stalling's hand.

We sit there together in silence, listening to the music from her transistor radio.

"I love this song," she says, turning up the volume. "Close to You" by the Carpenters plays, and I bob my head to the music, wishing I had enough nerve to ask her to dance. If I only knew how to dance, I probably would.

"Would you dance with me?" she asks.

"Sure." I stand, feet planted firmly on the ground, arms glued to my sides.

She giggles. "It would help if you put your arms around me."

A huge lump slides down my throat. I circle her shoulders, wishing I had taken a Fred Astaire class or something. Wherever people learn to dance. Once Mom tried to teach me the two-step in the kitchen, but I was a complete klutz.

Scarlett pushes my arms lower until they surround

her waist. Her hands lock together behind my neck, and she starts to move slowly in a circle. I follow her lead.

Even standing in bare feet, she's a few inches taller than me. My forehead tingles from barely touching her chin. Her skin is smooth as powder. I try to breathe in her scent, but I suddenly become aware of my sweat. If I knew I would have ever had a chance at dancing with Scarlett Stalling at Gossimer Lake tonight, I would have worn deodorant. I would have rolled a whole bottle over my entire body. Because just the sight of Scarlett Stalling makes me sweat. And now being this close to her, I'm sweating buckets.

"This is nice," she says. The way she says that in her sweet voice makes me remember to breathe. And in this moment I actually enjoy dancing with her to that song. Heck, we *are* that song. *Why do stars fall down from the sky every time you walk by? Just like me, they long to be close to you.*

"Ouch!" She releases me and jumps back.

"Did I step on your toes?"

"No." She slaps her arm. "Mosquitoes! When are they ever going to spray around Antler?"

Suddenly I feel them biting my ears, my cheeks, every inch of my exposed skin.

"I better go," she says. "Thanks for the dance, Toby.

You're great!" She leans over, kisses me on the cheek, picks up her radio, and dashes off.

I'm great. Me, Toby Wilson. Great. She said it. She even sealed it with a kiss. Or did she say it's late? No, she said *great*. I ride back home with Scarlett Stalling's kiss on my cheek, thinking how Wayne is right. Antler is the best place on the face of the earth.

Chapter Nine

I decide to mow the Pruitts' yard early because these days the temperature hits ninety degrees by noon. And I plan to spend the afternoon claiming the left side of Scarlett's swing.

The smell of fresh coffee drifts up to my bedroom. When I make my way downstairs, I'm surprised to see Dad at the kitchen table in his T-shirt and plaid pajama bottoms. Usually he's dressed for work by now. His hair sticks up and out like a mad scientist, and dark half-moons lurk below his eyes like he hasn't gotten a wink of sleep.

"Morning," he says, rolling the rubber band off the newspaper.

"Morning," I say, shuffling into the kitchen.

This is my first day at a real job—a job that has nothing to do with worms. I figure that deserves some sort of initiation. I pour coffee in Mom's Grand Ole Opry mug. Suddenly I feel numb, and it dawns on me why Dad looks lousy. Dancing with Scarlett clouded my thoughts, and I had forgotten about Mom—until now.

When I sit at the table, a small smile pulls at the corners of Dad's lips. "When did you start drinking coffee?"

I shrug, sort of embarrassed. "I don't know. This morning."

He picks up the sugar bowl. "Sugar?"

"Nah," I say.

He watches, waiting for me to sip. When I don't, he looks down at the newspaper. I lift the cup and take a big swallow. It burns.

Glancing at me over the paper, Dad smirks, then clears his throat and frowns, looking back at the paper as if he didn't notice me gagging. A moment later he says, "Do me a favor. Take that bucket of soil on the back porch over to Gloria. And give her that sack of tomatoes on the counter too."

Dad must feel rotten. Mrs. McKnight is one of the few people he enjoys talking to. She likes hearing about the optimum temperature for worms, and he likes learning about the different types of roses.

In Cal's backyard, Mrs. McKnight hangs underwear on the clothesline. Mom says Charlie McKnight is too stingy to fork out enough money for a clothes dryer. Every member of the McKnight family is represented on that line except Wayne. There's Cal's small Fruit of the Loom underwear, Billy's larger ones, and Mr. McKnight's boxers. Next to them hang pink polka-dotted and solid blue panties. Mrs. McKnight grabs a red bra from the plastic laundry basket and clips it to the line. I'm wondering if the bra is hers or Kate's when she peeks around the boxers and notices me staring at the bra. My whole body blushes.

Smiling, she says, "Oh, Toby, I didn't see you standing there."

I try to speak, but the words stick in my throat like cotton balls. All I can say is, "Err . . . uhh. Uhh—"

She glances down at the bucket. "Did your dad send me some of that terrific soil?" I think it's funny how people who like growing things call dirt "soil."

"Uhhh, yeah. Yes, ma'am."

She walks up to me and takes the bucket. "Thanks. I'll return your bucket later."

I hold out the sack, and she accepts it.

"These too?" She puts down the bucket and looks inside the sack. After taking a long whiff, she smiles. "Aaah. Fresh tomatoes. What a good neighbor. Tell your dad thank you for me." She takes a few steps, then stops. "My gracious, I almost forgot. How did your mother do last night?"

I'm not ready to explain because I'd have to confess I don't know when Mom will be back. "The Grand Ole Opry had a fire, and they postponed the contest."

"Oh, my goodness. Did anyone get hurt?"

"Oh, no, it only burned in the part where they were going to hold the contest."

Her forehead wrinkles. "Oh. Oh, well, I see."

"They haven't rescheduled it yet. Mom's hanging around till it's over."

Mrs. McKnight's smile makes my stomach knot up. "Well, wish her the best of luck for me when you speak to her."

I take off for the garage and wonder why I lied to Mrs. McKnight. She's the nicest person I've ever known, and I lied to her as easy as I did to my math teacher when I told him I forgot my homework. Only this lie makes me feel worse.

Miss Myrtie Mae's house is around the corner from ours on Cottonwood Street, so I don't have to drag the lawn mower very far. The Pruitt home is the biggest house in Antler. It stands green and tall behind two huge willow trees. Their house is the first one Cal and

I hit on our Halloween route. Every year Miss Myrtie Mae dresses like Glinda, the good witch in *The Wizard of Oz*, and gives out candy bars from the front porch. Her wrinkled face is a scary sight under that curly blond wig and rhinestone tiara, but it's worth looking at her and putting up with her Glinda speech in exchange for an Almond Joy.

Today Miss Myrtie Mae greets me at the door and tells me to wait in the living room with the Judge while she gets her list. I'm hoping it's short because of my big plans this afternoon at Scarlett's house.

The Judge sits there, fumbling with his pocket watch. Before Miss Myrtie Mae leaves the room, she says, "Brother, you remember Tobias Wilson, Opalina's boy? I'll be right back, Toby."

The Judge looks up, and stares at me. His head is cocked sideways and a string of drool hangs from the corner of his mouth.

Everything in the living room is either green or gold. Last year Miss Myrtie Mae hired a decorator from Amarillo to do over the entire house. Miss Myrtie Mae accidentally left the decorator's bill out when Miss Gladys Toodle was visiting. Ten thousand dollars. It was the talk of Antler until Christmas, when Miss Myrtie Mae and Miss Toodle competed with their outdoor decorations. They used so many outdoor lights, the entire town lost its electricity for a day.

Old black-and-white photos in silver frames crowd a round oak table near the couch. One is of two boys about my age in old-fashioned baseball uniforms. Another is of a pretty girl with a bow in her long dark curls. I figure they must be from the good-looking side of Miss Myrtie Mae's family.

I'm taking a closer look at the photos when the Judge says, "Young man."

I turn. He squints at me. "This is the last time I want to see you in this courtroom."

Glancing around, I realize he must be talking to me. "Judge, I think—"

He shakes his finger at me and the string of drool has grown longer, stretching past his chin. "Don't talk, son, when I'm handing down a verdict. I'm tired of this nonsense. Now you're going to have to do some time instead of paying a fine."

The front door is six feet behind me and I'm tempted to escape this crazy old man, but I've got a girl now, and I'll earn more money today than Dad has ever paid me.

The Judge stands, leaning heavy on his cane. "Young man, do you understand me?"

He inches toward me. I back toward the hall

and duck my head around the corner. "Uh, Miss Myrtie Mae?"

She returns, and it's the first time in my life I have been happy to see Miss Myrtie Mae Pruitt. The sight of the Judge breathing down my face doesn't fluster her at all. She pulls out a wadded tissue from her pocket and wipes his drool.

"Brother, this is Toby. He's our new lawn boy. Remember early this summer we had that nice McKnight boy, William? And I know you remember Wayne before that." She turns to me. "Brother loved Wayne. That youngest boy, though. He filled in for Billy once last year, and my heavens, you never saw such a mess—patches of tall grass, weeds left in the flower beds." She clicks her tongue. "We couldn't have that."

I feel bad for Cal. Maybe he *knew* the reason Miss Myrtie Mae didn't ask him to mow her yard this summer.

Miss Myrtie Mae hands me the list. Twenty-three tasks are marked on it, and I wonder how I'm ever going to see Scarlett before the sun sets.

"Come on," Miss Myrtie Mae says with a quick wave of her hand. Her pointed navy blue shoes tap against the wood floor.

I follow her into the backyard. As I scope out the grass carpet spread to eternity, I realize that the Pruitts not only have the largest house in Antler but they also have the biggest lawn. Morning glories spill over the back fence. A stone path winds its way to a white gazebo big enough for a high school band. Two apple trees' branches droop, heavy with apples, and the fruit litters the ground beneath them. I glance at the list.

#1: Pick up apples off the ground.

Miss Myrtie Mae points out the beds that need weeding. "Now, if you're ever in doubt if it's a weed or not, give me a holler. Better safe than sorry. I'll be in my darkroom." She leaves me alone in the yard.

Every green apple I pick up has a hole in it. I can't get away from worms. The vinegar smell of rotting apples on the ground makes me want to puke, and roly-polies invade the fruit like an army climbing over green mountains.

#2: Mow lawn in an east-west pattern.

The yard seems to go on forever. East to west. West to east. The mower roars and spits grass blades to the side. The smell of freshly cut grass fills the air. Halfway through the job, I decide mowing isn't boring if you make your own designs. I make a circle, a square, then a triangle. Nothing to it, so I move on to more complicated forms. I zigzag along the fence. I make curlicues. I begin to spell Scarlett. I—see Miss Myrtie Mae peeking out her window, frowning at me. I stop in the middle of my letter *S*. East to west. West to east.

About the time I finish mowing, Miss Myrtie Mae comes outside, carrying a silver tray with a glass pitcher of iced tea, some lemon drop cookies, and jiggly lime Jell-O stuff. She must think we're going to have a tea party. Sheriff Levi follows her, his head and shoulders drooping, like a kid ordered to go to church. Seeing him makes me think about Zachary, and I wonder what the sheriff will do if Paulie Rankin doesn't return.

"I reckon you deserve a break by now," Miss Myrtie Mae says. Her bun is loose, and wiry gray strands stick out around her face. "Sheriff Levi happened by at the right time."

Sheriff Levi wears a pair of plaid shorts, a yellow knit shirt, and his lucky fishing hat decorated with tackle. "Well, actually, Miss Myrtie Mae, I just came by to ask Toby something." I'm willing to bet he wants worms.

Miss Myrtie Mae acts like she can't hear him and

proceeds down the stone path. "Let's sit in the gazebo, where there is plenty of shade."

She sits in the white rocker and motions the sheriff and me to the chairs around the wicker table. I collapse in one of them, but Sheriff Levi keeps standing. He glances at his watch, and his eye twitches. "Miss Myrtie Mae, this must be such an inconvenience, me barging in on you and all. I really just want to get some—"

"Nonsense!" Miss Myrtie Mae says. "Now sit!"

"Worms," he says as his rear end meets the chair.

"It's too hot to eat anything warm, so I made my lime gelatin turkey salad." She slices a piece of the wiggly stuff onto a china plate and hands it to me. My stomach feels queasy at the sight of turkey chunks floating inside lime Jell-O. I glance at Sheriff Levi, and the way his eye twitches studying the Jell-O, I figure he feels the same way.

I'm sweaty and not sure Miss Myrtie Mae would approve of me using her nice fancy napkin to wipe the sweat from my forehead. I don't know what to do with that napkin, and I watch Sheriff Levi, but he doesn't seem to know either. So I wait for Miss Myrtie Mae's cue. She flings hers open and drops it daintily into her lap. The sheriff and I follow her lead, only when

I fling my napkin, one corner lands in the pitcher of iced tea. I go to rescue it, only to knock my glass of ice over.

"Whoa, whoa, Toby," she says. "Sit back. I'll get you a clean glass of ice." I want to tell her don't bother. I'm filthy and sweaty, and dirty ice won't hurt me at this point. In fact, any kind of ice sounds great, but she swiftly removes the glass and disappears into her house.

Sheriff Levi leans over the table and whispers fast, "Toby, can I help myself to some worms? I'm heading out to my secret fishing hole."

"Sure, Sheriff, help yourself."

"I'll leave the money in the tin can."

"No problem." Dad leaves an empty coffee can on the shelf so the locals can take what they need and leave the money in case we're not there, but Sheriff Levi always hunts us down before taking any.

Miss Myrtie Mae heads our way with my glass of ice, so I quickly ask, "Sheriff, what could happen to Zachary Beaver if Paulie Rankin doesn't come back?"

Sheriff Levi tips back his hat. "I'll have to notify social services in Amarillo."

"What does that mean?"

He tries to steady his eye by raising his brows. He removes his hat and wipes the sweat off his forehead with a handkerchief. "He'll probably be put in a foster home or some sort of home for juveniles."

"Oh." I look away. Some blurry white moths fly by, their wings fluttering in the breeze. I don't like Zachary Beaver, but I don't much like the thought of him living in some house with strangers either.

Miss Myrtie Mae hands me the fresh glass of ice. "Here you go, Toby."

Sheriff Levi shovels the salad into his mouth in quick huge bites, then washes it down with iced tea, holding his head back as he empties the glass. Giant gulps move down his throat, then he stands and announces, "Miss Myrtie Mae, I hate to eat and run, but I forgot Duke was waiting for me in the car." He grabs a couple of lemon drop cookies, tips his hat, and steps off the gazebo before Miss Myrtie Mae can utter a protest.

Four hours later I sack up the grass, then cross off task number twenty-three. The flower beds are groomed and free of weeds. I feel proud. I'm different than Cal—I finish projects. I remember when Cal and I were five or six and we turned on the garden hose and made a mess in the mud. Wayne fetched Cal and cleaned him from head to toe with the hose before taking him into the house. I cleaned myself off. I don't have big brothers watching out for me.

Before paying me, Miss Myrtie Mae inspects the yard. She walks to each corner flower bed. Her eyes comb every grass blade, and when she spots an apple on the ground, she walks over and picks it up. It probably fell a second ago.

She hands me my money and says in a sharp voice, "Not bad, but next time take care in the direction you mow. You shock the grass blades if you don't cut it in an east-to-west pattern. Can I expect you next week?"

My arms ache from pushing the lawn mower, my back throbs from bending over picking up apples, and my hands have blisters on them from pulling weeds. I open my mouth and say, "Yes, ma'am."

Miss Myrtie Mae asks me to step inside the house for a moment, and I'm relieved that the Judge isn't inside, waiting to haul me off to prison. Smells of something wonderful drift from the kitchen. The TV is on, and the early evening news broadcasts from a jungle in Vietnam. I wonder if Wayne is nearby.

Miss Myrtie Mae shakes her head, looking at the television. "Oh, that mess! I hope you never have to see war, Toby. Our poor Wayne. I include him in my prayers each and every night." She looks up at me like she has just thought of another list of chores for me to do. "Toby, almost forgot about your mom. How'd she shake out?"

I don't even hesitate. "The place where they were going to hold the contest had a fire, so they—"

Her eyebrows shoot up. "The Grand Ole Opry burned down?"

"Uh, it was only a small fire, but they postponed the contest. She's waiting around until they reschedule it." I'm turning into a full-fledged pathological liar.

Miss Myrtie Mae lowers her eyebrows and frowns. I study the rug covering her wood floor. "That a fact?" she asks. "Hold on. I'll be right back." She walks into the kitchen, and I wonder if she's calling Dad to check if I'm telling the truth. But a moment later she returns with a pan covered with aluminum foil. "Would you mind taking this German chocolate cake over to Mr. Beaver's place? He mentioned a fondness for chocolate."

I leave with the pan, wondering how I'll manage to get it and the lawn mower home without dropping it. I also wonder how much daylight is left before my plans to see Scarlett sink fast below the horizon. As soon as I clean up, I'm going straight to Scarlett's. Mr. Zachary Beaver will have to wait for his cake.

As I reach the bottom step of the Pruitts' front porch, I hear a creak. "Stop right there, young man."

I swirl around. The Judge leans forward in a porch rocker, shaking his cane at me. "You remember what I said, you hear?"

Chapter Ten

Tired to the bone, I arrive home around five o'clock and head for the shower. Mom used to nag me about washing places like my elbows or the back of my neck. Not today. When I step out of the shower, my skin feels raw from scrubbing every inch.

A towel wrapped around me, I lean into the mirror and examine my upper lip. Fuzz. I wonder if whiskers are like pimples and that one morning I'll wake up with a face covered with them. I splash on some of Dad's Royal Copenhagen aftershave. And today I use deodorant.

Before leaving, I stick a note on the refrigerator with a magnet telling Dad I'll be home for dinner. Then I take off for Scarlett's house.

All the homes on Scarlett's street look pretty much alike—tiny with single garages and small yards surrounded by link fences. But one has a wooden porch swing with the left side reserved for me.

At Scarlett's house I hide the German chocolate cake between a bush and the fence. Since Miss Myrtie Mae covered the top with aluminum foil, it should be safe until I take it over to Zachary.

Scarlett is exactly as I pictured her, sitting on the porch, her long legs stretched across the swing. A magazine rests in her lap, and she's so engrossed in it, she doesn't see me.

Before I step through the gate, Tara and three other little kids march past me in a line. Upside-down plastic plant pots perch on top of their heads. Tara, the leader of the pack, has about seven vacation Bible school ribbons pinned to her shirt. Moist wisps of hair cling to her sunburned face.

She walks up to me and says, "We're having a parade, and I'm the mayor. And they're the Shiners." This kid grows weirder by the minute.

"You mean *Shriners*," I say.

"That's what I said. Shiners."

I ignore the brat and slow my pace toward Scarlett. No reason to seem too eager. It spoils the image. Scarlett is thumbing through her magazine, popping her chewing gum, and doesn't notice me until I step onto the porch. She looks up and smiles, her lips shiny with lip gloss. "Hey. How ya doing?"

Oxygen leaves my body in one big *whoosh*. "Fine."

I remember to breathe again, only I suck up too much air and start coughing. I cover my mouth and try to swallow, but it's no use.

"You okay?" she asks. "Do you need a glass of water?"

Holding up my palm, I manage to say, "I'm fine." I wish I could start all over—opening the gate, repeating my slow cool walk toward the porch, maybe a casual lift of my eyebrows when she says hi.

But Scarlett doesn't seem to mind. Her gaze slides over the magazine page and she sighs. "You know, there's a whole world out there waiting in the back of magazines."

"Hmm? You mean in the ads?"

"Yeah. Didn't you ever want anything in the back of a magazine?"

"Well, I always wanted to order those sea monkeys in the Superman comics. But my dad said they were a waste of money."

She laughs. "Sea monkeys?"

I feel my face go red. I decide not to mention the Atlas Body Building course.

"I mean these kind of ads." She points to an ad

about a modeling school in Dallas right next to one about becoming a stewardess. The wind blows her hair across her face, and a few strands stick to her lip gloss. She swings her feet to the porch floor and scoots over, leaving room for me on the right. It's not the left, where Juan sat, but I guess it really doesn't matter.

Leaving a foot of space between us, I sit next to her and take deep breaths. Her hair smells like flowers.

I want to hold Scarlett's hand, but mine are sweaty. I should have used deodorant on them. Maybe one day I'll invent a hand deodorant and market it to guys like me who want to get rid of their wet palms.

"Is that what you want to be?" I ask. "A model?"

"Maybe, if I can get these fixed." She taps on her two front teeth.

"What's wrong with your smile?" I know she's talking about the gap, but I love her gap.

She sighs. "Oh, Toby. You have to be perfect to be a model. And I'd look better without it. See?" She smiles, and a piece of chewing gum fills the space.

I shrug.

"Or maybe a stewardess. That would be the next best thing, to fly around the world. How glamorous."

I'd ridden in a plane once when we flew to my grandmother's funeral. The stewardesses served drinks, handed out peanuts, and asked if we had any garbage. A little kid threw up on one of them. But I decide not to mention any of that.

She tucks a strand of hair behind her ear. "Of course, to be an international stewardess, I'd have to know another language." She says *international stewardess* like it's as official as a U.S. ambassador job. "Juan was helping me learn Spanish before . . ." She gazes into the yard.

I should have listened to Dad and enrolled in Spanish class last year instead of shop. He told me learning a foreign language would come in handy. Just as I start to scooch toward her, Scarlett stands, stretching her arms above her head. "I've got to cook dinner. Mom will be home from work any minute. You can come in if you want."

If I want? Yes, I want. I follow her into her house, which is dark and smells musty like an attic. Clothes cover shabby furniture and toys litter the floor. Scarlett breezes into the kitchen, dodging the whole mess. I stub my toe on a giant baby doll with batches of hair torn out.

Scarlett fills a pot with water. "Toby, would you get my radio? It's in my room."

I glance around for a door.

"Go down the hall. It's the first door on the right."

In the room, two unmade twin beds have matching floral bedspreads, but it's as if there is an imaginary line drawn down the middle of the floor. One side has a ton of stuffed animals and dolls without arms and heads. I swear Tara is headed for the women's penitentiary.

The other side of the room has Bobby Sherman posters taped on every square inch of the wall. I remember signing the Autograph Hound sitting at the head of her bed. It was the last day of school. I should have written something great like *Peace* or *Stay cool*. But I signed, *See you next year, Toby Wilson*.

I walk over to her dresser and pick up a cologne bottle. Wind Song. My hands shake, but I remove the cap anyway and smell it. The smell is faint, so I spray a little on my hand and take a close sniff.

"Ummm!" Tara stands in the doorway, the plant

pot gone from her head. "Scarlett, Toby's spraying your perfume!"

I put down the bottle, grab the radio off her dresser, and head out. My face burns, and I know the scent gives me away.

Scarlett drops pasta in the water while I wipe my hand on my jeans.

With hands on her hips, Tara says, "Toby tried your perfume."

Shaking my head, I talk fast. "I knocked the bottle over when I grabbed the radio. Then the top fell off and I put it back."

"Na-ah!" Tara says. "You sprayed on some perfume!"

"Oh, Tara," Scarlett says. "Scram."

The phone rings and Scarlett lunges for it, picking up the receiver before it finishes the first ring. There's no denying it. This girl has answered many phone calls.

"What do you want?" she says into the phone. "It's Juan," she mouths.

Tara pulls at my shirt. "I want to see him again."

Ignoring Tara, I try to hear Scarlett's every word and not look interested. I watch the pot of water boil.

Scarlett sighs. "I don't want to talk to you." She sounds cold, almost mean, but I'm thinking, Yeah, cool, she doesn't want to talk to you.

Tara tugs at my shirt again. "I want to see *him*!"

"I have company," Scarlett tells Juan.

Yeah, Juan, I think, go lick your wounds. She's got a new man.

"Who?" Scarlett glances my way.

I swallow.

"Toby Wilson."

Why did she have to say that? My stomach dribbles like a basketball. I see Juan towering over me with his number-five iron. I should have sent off for that Atlas Body Building course.

"Don't call back." Scarlett hangs up the phone. She bites her lower lip and tears fill her eyes.

"What's wrong?" I ask, reaching for her arm.

But Scarlett steps away from my touch, shakes her head, fumbles through a drawer, and grabs a can opener. "Nothing."

It doesn't matter. I already know. It's the words she's etched all over her notebooks since fifth grade— *Scarlett Stalling loves Juan Garcia*.

Tara stomps her feet. "I WANT TO SEE THE FAT MAN AGAIN!"

"Tara, stop screaming!" yells Scarlett. She sighs, and her voice softens. "Toby, would you mind?"

"No," I lie. "Not at all." I leave the girl of my dreams in the kitchen, pining over some other guy, while I take her possessed sister to see Zachary Beaver. Loser is my middle name.

When Zachary Beaver Came to Town

KIMBERLY WILLIS HOLT

Zachary Beaver, the fattest boy in the world, comes to town and changes the lives of everyone in Antler, Texas—especially that of thirteen-year-old Toby Wilson.

IN THE CLASSROOM

This coming-of-age story is both humorous and poignant, making it a perfect choice for class read-aloud or a novel study. Kimberly Willis Holt clearly understands the feelings of a thirteen-year-old boy and deals honestly with topics such as death, war, and obesity.

The themes of *family, abandonment, friendship, self-discovery,* and *bullying/rudeness* will guide readers to a better understanding of the important things that affect a person's life. In addition to discussion questions related to the themes, this guide provides activities that link language arts, social studies, science, music, and art.

107

Have students create a list of the things they have in common with their best friend and the things they may disagree on. Ask them what the phrase *unlikely friendship* means. Discuss the fact that sometimes people from different backgrounds can still be friends. How might an unlikely friendship change a person's life?

THEMATIC CONNECTIONS

FRIENDSHIP—Toby and Cal have been friends for a long time. How does Cal need Toby when Wayne dies? Discuss whether Cal is more upset with Toby because of the letter he wrote Wayne or because Toby didn't attend Wayne's funeral. At what point in the novel do Toby and Cal begin to see Zachary as a friend? Why does it take Zachary so long to warm up to the boys?

FAMILY—How is Toby's relationship with his parents different from the relationships in Cal's family? Describe Toby's feelings for Wayne, Cal's brother. Why does Toby write a letter to Wayne and sign Cal's name? Reread the dialogue between Toby and his dad (pp.192–197). How do Mr. Wilson's words explain what has happened to their family? Does this talk help Toby better understand his father and the decisions he has made?

◎ **ABANDONMENT**—Toby, Cal, and Zachary Beaver have all been abandoned in some way. Ask students to compare and contrast the way each boy deals with his loss. How do they help each other? Toby says, "For a little person Mom sure leaves a hole" (p. 48). Discuss whether Toby's decision to read all the unread letters from his mother is symbolic of his acceptance that she isn't coming home.

◎ **SELF-DISCOVERY**—Toby says, "Loser is my middle name" (p. 107). Why does he see himself as a loser? Ask students to chart Toby's changes from the beginning of the novel to the end. What does he learn about himself? Discuss Zachary's role in Toby's self-discovery.

◎ **BULLYING/RUDENESS**—When Zachary Beaver rolls into town, people shout things like "Fatty, fatty, two by four," and ask embarrassing questions like "How much do you eat?" Discuss whether these are the words of bullies or simply rude people. Why is Toby so sensitive to the way Zachary is treated? Discuss how Zachary deals with it.

INTERDISCIPLINARY CONNECTIONS

LANGUAGE ARTS—Have students write the letter that Toby decides to write to his mom. What does he tell her about the summer? What does he say about her leaving home? What does he say about himself?

Ask students to select a book that Toby and Cal might put in the Antler Library in honor of Zachary. Have students write an appropriate inscription for the book.

SOCIAL STUDIES—The novel takes place during the Vietnam War. Ask students to research the years during which the Vietnam War occurred and who the presidents were during this time. Freddy, the bait shop owner, tells Toby that he fought in World War II. He says, "Back then, we came back heroes" (p. 124). Ask students to research the years during which World War II took place. Discuss with the class the different circumstances of these wars and what Freddy meant by his comment.

Ask students to use the Internet to find out the history of circus sideshows. Why do some people call these shows freak shows? How are such freak shows an exploitation of people with abnormalities?

SCIENCE—Toby says that most farms in his area of Texas use herbicides to control weeds and insecticides to get rid of bugs. Ask students to find out the most common herbicides and insecticides that farmers use to protect their crops. What is the danger in using such products? Have students find out the safest methods of protecting crops.

MUSIC—Toby's mother left home to pursue a career in country music. Bring in recordings of country music from the 1960s and from today. Play the music for the class and ask students to draw comparisons between the styles of songs from the two decades.

VOCABULARY/USE OF LANGUAGE

The vocabulary of the book is not difficult, but students may find some unfamiliar words that they should try to define, using clues from the context of the story. Such words may include *octaves* (p. 79), *optimum* (p. 85), *dinghy* (p. 192), and *concordance* (p. 207).

Belle Prater's Boy
Ruth White
- Self-discovery
- Family
- Friendship
- Abandonment

Grades 5 up / 0-440-41372-9

Journey
Patricia MacLachlan
- Family
- Friendship
- Abandonment
- Self-discovery

Grades 4 up / 0-440-40809-1

Blubber
Judy Blume
- Self-discovery
- Bullying
- Friendship

Grades 4–6 / 0-440-90707-1

Find a Stranger, Say Goodbye
Lois Lowry
- Self-discovery
- Family
- Abandonment

Grades 6 up / 0-440-20541-7

Prepared by Pat Scales, Director of Library Services, South Carolina Governor's School for the Arts and Humanities, Greenville

ABOUT THE AUTHOR

The daughter of a navy chief, **Kimberly Willis Holt** attended schools all over the world. Her address changed every couple of years, although two things remained the same—her love of reading good books and her dream of becoming a writer. Ms. Holt says, "Although I read and loved books that many other girls enjoyed, such as *Little Women* and the Laura Ingalls Wilder books, it was Carson McCullers' *The Heart Is a Lonely Hunter* that inspired me to write. Her characters are so real they leap off the page."

Fuqua Photography, Inc.

Ms. Holt also credits her upbringing with nurturing her desire to write. "I come from a family of storytellers. Maybe it has something to do with being Southern, but conversations with my parents and grandparents are filled with vibrant details and fascinating people. You don't just listen to what they are saying, you experience it. I believe their tales hooked me into the storytelling process at an early age."

For years Ms. Holt put her dream on hold, working as a radio news director and in various marketing jobs. Then one day she picked up a pen and yellow pad and started writing her first book, *My Louisiana Sky*. The inspiration had been with her for a long time.

When Kimberly Willis Holt was thirteen, she saw the Fattest Boy in the World at the Louisiana State Fair. "I'm afraid I was like Cal, asking a million nosy questions," the author says of her experience. This strong memory gave her the idea for *When Zachary Beaver Came to Town*.

Having lived all over the world, Kimberly Willis Holt now resides in Amarillo, Texas, with her husband, Jerry, and their daughter, Shannon.

PRAISE FOR
Summer Soldiers

"A fascinating snapshot of the times."
—*School Library Journal*

"Lindquist's characters contend with many thorny issues—friendship, bravery, and bullies—in a realistic yet upbeat manner."   —*Booklist*

"Interesting and profound. . . . Joe and Jim emerge as true-to-life heroes embodying many different levels of courage."   —*Publishers Weekly*

"Tender. . . . This is WWI from a boy's perspective, relayed in homespun language that is surprisingly effective."   —*Kirkus Reviews*

SUMMER
SOLDIERS

◆

SUSAN HART LINDQUIST

A Yearling Book

Published by
Dell Yearling
an imprint of
Random House Children's Books
a division of Random House, Inc.
1540 Broadway
New York, New York 10036

To order classroom sets of
Summer Soldiers (ISBN 0-440-41537-3) in paperback,
please contact your local distributor or bookstore.

Promotional copy—not for sale

Visit us on the Web! www.randomhouse.com/kids
Educators and librarians, for a variety of teaching tools,
visit us at www.randomhouse.com/teachers

ISBN 0-440-41537-3

Reprinted by arrangement with Delacorte Press

Printed in the United States of America

July 2000

OPM

FOR MY PARENTS
AND FOR MGMFB
AND HERS

ONLY WHEN WE RESPECT A MAN'S RIGHT TO CHOOSE
DO WE TRULY RESPECT HIS FREEDOM.

CHAPTER I

SURE THING, IT WASN'T US who caused the trouble. Nobody could have said we were doing anything but minding our own business, Jim and Luther and Billy and me—just sitting peaceful on that fence, kicking our boots against the rail and waiting to be called over to the picnic tables for dinner.

The long, hot, dusty day was finally rolling on into twilight, that red August sun hanging lazy in the treetops across the river. We were all enjoying the way the breeze from the ocean was coming up behind us over Morgan's horse pasture, cooling our sunburned necks.

The four of us were just relaxing and congratulating ourselves for the hard work we'd put in helping our daddies on the sheep drive, when right out of nowhere a soggy old horse apple came zooming through the air and hit Luther splat on the forehead.

We all leaped off that fence quick as hop-toads.

"It's them," Jim Morgan said, crouching low as another manure rocket whizzed by. "It's Harley and those other two lousy brothers of yours, Luther."

"Who else *would* it be?" Luther said. "They've been waiting all day for a chance to get us."

Up till then it had been a fine day. In fact, it had been a regular celebration of wild times. We'd worked hard, whooping those sheep over the hill to Maxwell like regular drovers, them flowing along easy as water without straying off even once. And there'd been no trouble with Luther's brothers since we'd taken care to keep our daddies between us and them.

Yep, it had been a fine time all around. No trouble with the Thornton boys, no trouble with the sheep. We'd gotten a good price for our lambs, and for a change there'd been no talk of the war.

I looked over at Luther. A big green splot of manure was dripping down the side of his face. I couldn't help but laugh.

"What you grinning at, Joe?" He whacked me on the arm, then wiped his cheek with his sleeve. "You don't look so pretty yourself." Sure enough, I'd taken a hit on my shoulder.

Another volley of manure bombs came hurtling our way. Billy ducked, checking the back of his shirt. He made a good target with all that red hair of his. "Where are they? You see them?"

We peered through the fence rails.

"There!" Jim said, pointing toward the big cottonwood tree out in the pasture.

All three of Luther's big brothers—Harley and Ray and Arlo—came strolling out from behind the tree, innocent as newborn lambs, acting as if they hadn't done a thing.

Sure there were four of us and only three of them, but they were older and more muscled up than any of us eleven-year-olds. Luther's oldest brother, Harley, was sixteen and built like he'd been a lumberjack all his life. Ray was short but bulldog mean, and Arlo was near as mean, just maybe not as quick and smart. But *we* were smart. Smart enough to know not to take them on.

"We could make a run for it," Billy said.

I guess we could have. Our mamas were there just across the yard setting dinner out on the tables, and our daddies were there too, talking by the fire. If we could get to them we'd be safe.

But that patch of ground between us and our parents might as well have been that bloody battlefield called no-man's-land way over there in Europe.

"Here they come," said Billy, backing up against the fence.

They were passing through the gate and walking around to our side.

"Whoa, now!" Harley said, stopping to point at us. "Look there! It's the Hobby Horse Gang. Looks like they've been riding the wrong end of their horses."

"That Harley's a bigger bully than the German Kaiser," Billy mumbled, soft, so none of them could hear.

Might not have been quite *that* bad, but I swear, no group of boys ever had a stronger talent for tormentation.

All three of them busted up laughing at the sight of

us, hunkered down there by the fence all decorated and stunk up with manure.

Right then I figured it sure would have been nice if all those boys were old enough to get drafted. Maybe somebody'd even send them over to France so they could get themselves shot by those Germans.

"Ha!" said Ray. "Look there at Luther. Looks like little brother and his friends messed themselves!"

"I'm telling you!" Harley said, taking a wide step around us, sniffing the air. "Smells like it too!"

"Ah, they stink, all right," said Ray. "Just as bad as usual!"

"You tykes need a good wash," Arlo said.

"Naw," said Harley. "Leave 'em be. The flies'll clean them off. Come on, let's go get some food."

The three of them started off across the grass toward the picnic area.

Now, I'm of the mind that things might have died down after that, if Luther had stayed put. But that wasn't Luther's way. I guess he decided he'd had enough. He stood up and started after them.

I yanked on his pant leg. "Stay down," I said. "Stay down and they'll leave us alone."

But Luther didn't listen. He pulled away and headed straight out across the yard.

"Hey!" he yelled.

Ever since we were big enough to matter to Harley and those boys, Jim and Billy and I'd done our best to steer clear of them—just to avoid losing any blood. But not Luther. Once he got going, he'd egg his three big brothers on with his sassy mouth just like he *wanted* to get kicked around.

"We going to stop him?" Billy asked, looking over at me. Trail dirt had dusted out all his freckles, but I could still see worry in his eyes.

Jim looked sort of worried too.

"Face-to-face!" Luther shouted at his brothers again, making his hands into fists. He was getting way too excited. "Any one of you! Face-to-face!"

Billy and Jim gave me that worried look again.

"Hey, Luther!" I shouted at him.

"Come on, Luther," Billy said. "Knock it off. You're going to get us all killed."

Luther just grinned back at us. Then he did an about-face, cupped his hands around his mouth, and shouted, "What are you, Harley? Chicken or something?"

Like they were lined up ready to do a dance together, those big Thornton boys turned all three at the same time.

Jim looked at me. I looked at Jim. Billy said, "Uh-oh"; then the three of us scrambled over the fence.

"We'll see who's chicken!" Harley called back, coming fast across the field.

Quick as that, those boys had a hold on Luther. Even quicker they dragged him over the grass and dunked him headfirst in the watering trough.

That's about the time Luther's daddy finally noticed what was going on. He came charging across the yard like a bee-stung bull.

"Quit!" Mr. Thornton shouted, grabbing Ray and Arlo by the back of their shirts. He yelled at Harley to leave Luther and the rest of us alone. "You get to that table and help your mama!" His face had gone hot poker red and he looked angry enough to chew bullets. Arlo was the only one slow enough to get a hard kick in the rear end with Mr. Thornton's boot.

Considering that boot and his daddy's expression, Luther could have done a whole lot more thinking just then. He would have been smart to hold his tongue. But as usual, he spoke up like no one else was around. "Yeah, you stupid hens!" he yelled at his brothers. "Go help Mama!"

Luther's daddy came swooping down on him like a hawk and shook him so hard water came flying out of his ears. "*You* button that lip, mister, or you'll get worse from me than they *ever* gave you!" Mr. Thornton plopped Luther down hard on the ground, then left him there and stomped off, so mad you could practically see steam rising from his head.

Papa and the other men joined us then, and we climbed back over the fence.

Jim's daddy gave Luther a hand up off the ground. "You all right, son?"

"Sure, Mr. Morgan. I'm okay."

"You too, Jim?" his daddy asked.

"I'm all right, Pa. We're all fine."

"I wonder what comes over those boys," Papa said as he brushed off my sleeve.

Mr. Teale nodded, dampening his handkerchief in the trough and wiping Billy's face.

Papa shook his head. "I wonder why they can't seem to leave you boys alone."

Papa wondered about everything. He spoke that way, all the time starting sentences with, "I wonder . . . ," then ending with something like ". . . what the moon is made of" or ". . . why the sky is blue" or ". . . why they can't seem to leave you boys alone."

"I don't know," I said. "I wonder about that too."

"They're not so tough," Luther said, pretending as usual that he could have handled them.

If I'd spoken for myself I'd have said I was mighty glad our daddies showed up to keep those Thornton boys from licking us as good as I knew they could. Just like the French and those other folks in Europe were probably saying hearty thanks to us for helping to save them from the Germans.

NEARLY ALL THE DAYLIGHT was gone, and across the yard bugs were coming up around the lanterns on the tables.

Papa and I walked over to join Mama and the others. I tried to slick back my hair when I saw Jim's sister, Claire, walking across the grass carrying a platter of biscuits. She was dressed up clean and fresh as a meadow. My little sisters, Alice and Helen, were tagging along after her. Their voices came floating over the pasture with the sound of waking crickets.

"It's been a long day, Joe," Papa said, laying his hand on my shoulder. "Let's try to keep the peace."

"I'll do my best," I said.

Our mamas took care of that—sat us with Alice and Helen at a different table from Luther's brothers—so we kept the peace pretty easy during dinner. More so than our daddies, that's a sure thing. Straightaway they got to talking about the war, same as they'd been doing for the last three years, ever since 1914 when it began.

But I have to say, I didn't blame them. It was all mighty exciting. Heck, soon as President Wilson finally got us into the war last April, you couldn't take two steps down Main Street without seeing a flag, or a billboard shouting out "Buy War Bonds!" or "Enlist!" Sometimes Luther and Jim and Billy and I would get to talking about maybe going over there too, to fight like the heroes from the war biographies we'd been made to read in school—stories about the brave lives of George Washington and Joan of Arc. We talked big about being ace bomber pilots or doughboys charging out of those trenches and crossing into no-man's-land to take on the German army.

Our daddies talked big too, and they were stirring up some commotion at their table, all their voices blending into one, getting riled about the war.

"I'd like to give those lousy Huns a piece of my mind!"

"Ought to join up and go after that Kaiser Wilhelm ourselves!"

"You bet! That coward'd be no match for us!"

"Sure enough. We'd finish up over there and be back home by Christmas!"

Luther's daddy was getting so agitated that he had to

get up and start pacing around the table, kicking up dust with his boots.

"Hell, yes!" he said. "No disputing we've waited long enough!"

Right then Mrs. Thornton pulled him back down into his seat and the rest of the women set into changing the subject of conversation.

AFTER DINNER WE ALL SAT around the fire—all of us but those big Thornton boys. They just sort of stayed lurking at the edges of the circle like a nervous pack of wolves.

Our dog, Spit, came sidling up to Papa and lay down across his knee so he could pick the ticks out of her fur. Papa looked across the fire to where I was sitting with the fellows.

"You boys did fine today," he said. "Put in a good day's work."

"It was a fine day all around," I said, nodding. "We'll do it again next year, won't we?"

"Sheep have to get to market. Sure enough we'll be counting on all you boys to help. You and the dogs," he said, ruffling Spit's fur. She rolled over and let him scratch her stomach.

Spit had worked hard alongside the Thornton dogs, Ben and Pete. Between our four families we only had those three. The Teales never had a dog because Billy's mama said they made her sneeze. The Morgans used to have one until last spring, when she got herself kicked in the head by Mr. Morgan's best mare.

I looked over at Jim's daddy and remembered how he'd walked away after that pup died, cradling the poor thing like she was a newborn baby, blood spilling out the side of her mouth and all over Mr. Morgan's arm. Jim told me his daddy'd said later that he'd never own another dog as long as he had horses, even if it made him dependent on the rest of us when it came to working the sheep. I was glad of that, though. Kept our families together so we could have good times like these.

I went back to enjoying the evening, lazing by the fire.

Mr. Teale unpacked his guitar and we sang for a while, "Foggy, Foggy Dew" and "Red River Valley" being the only ones the boys and I really pitched in on. After that, Papa offered to give a recitation like he did every year after the drive. As a closing to the day, he said. Mama chose to hear Longfellow's "The Village Blacksmith," which I liked a whole lot better coming from Papa than I had when I read it in school.

When he finished, everyone was quiet until Mr. Teale stood up and tossed another log on the fire. "'Thus at the flaming forge of life,'" he said, repeating a line of the poem, "'our fortunes must be wrought . . .'"

Mr. Thornton sat forward and poked the fire with a stick. "No good fortune in that war," he said. "It's a sorry life they're living over there." Sparks crackled into the night sky.

"Too many wounded," said Papa, leaning to one side to take his knife out of his pocket. "Too many dead.

Too many starving children." When he picked up a stick to start whittling, I knew he was doing some serious thinking. "It's so difficult to understand," he said.

He was right. Everything about the war was hard to understand. Sure, I'd learned that America was fighting to save Democracy and to keep the German soldiers from coming over here, but it still didn't make much sense to me.

"Can't deny those Brits could use a bigger hand," Billy's daddy said.

Papa turned to Mr. Morgan. "What do you think, George?"

"Can't say as I know," he said. "It's all so blasted confusing." He stood up then, and walked away from the fire.

"Where's your daddy going?" I asked Jim.

"Ah, you know Pa. He's probably going out to check on the horses."

That would be like Mr. Morgan. Jim's daddy spent all the time he could with his horses—more than with human beings, I imagine.

"It's time we talked about it," Luther's daddy said.

"Maybe it's time we did more than talk," said Mr. Teale.

Mr. Thornton reached to stir the fire again.

Papa was whittling on, slowly, carefully.

"Probably our duty," Mr. Teale said.

"Yes," said Papa. "Perhaps. Perhaps it *is* the right thing to do."

Jim's mama looked across the fire toward us boys. In the firelight I saw her eyes turn, catching hold of

Mama. I looked at my mother. Her eyes were holding just as hard back on Mrs. Morgan.

Till that moment it had never occurred to me our daddies would really decide to go off and fight in the war. Never once, in fact. With wives and kids and being married so long, every single one of them was exempt from the service. None of them got drafted like what was happening to all the younger fellows in town.

I'd heard a million times that women and children were being burned and murdered in their houses over there. Heard it so many times I could recite it in my sleep. Heard that the Belgians were starving. That if we didn't help, the world would come to ruin.

Still, before that night, I never imagined my papa going—actually signing up to meet those Germans face-to-face. But he did.

2

BY MORNING, ALL OUR DADDIES had decided to enlist. All of them except Jim's. Mr. Morgan said he wouldn't be going. Said his heart just wasn't in the fight. He didn't need to be a hero, he said.

I don't know if being a hero was what Papa had in mind. If it was, he sure never said so to me. Heck, for the days before he left all he talked about was some box he'd lost. He went around wondering and worrying about it, taking me aside to ask if I'd seen it.

"An old cookie tin," he said, "with a blue willow pattern. It's one my daddy gave me to keep special things in. Sharing a room with those brothers of mine, all the privacy I ever had in the world fit inside that box."

I didn't have the slightest idea why he thought finding it was so important, but wondering about it occupied his mind clear up till the night before he went away.

That evening he and I went out to walk off the big

dinner of fricassee and biscuits Mama'd made special since he was leaving. We turned up our collars and headed out toward the place where we liked to sit and talk—the ridge above our house where an old grove of cypress trees leaned against the wind. It was an especially nice spot, a flat piece of ground with a view of the valley clear to the ocean, and with two decently comfortable rocks for us to sit on.

Papa whistled for Spit to join us. She didn't like me much, but I felt sort of sorry for her anyhow. Papa was the only human on earth she cared one whit about, and she didn't even know he was leaving. She trotted along just like it was any other after-dinner walk.

We hiked up the hill without talking, but when Papa stopped to gaze out over the valley, something told me that old box was still sitting as heavy on his mind as Mama's biscuits were on our stomachs.

"Wonder if I buried it somewhere," he said.

He bent to pick a stick up off the ground before he sat down. Then he took out his jackknife. I watched the way he opened that knife, his barbed-wire-scarred fingers carefully pulling back the blade, then turning it to make it bear down on the rough bark of the stick. He curled off a clean white ribbon of wood, let it fall, then brought the blade back to pull off another, then another. Spit went scooting after the whittling chips as they scattered in the wind.

"What's so special about that box?" I asked. "What's inside?"

For just a moment, he glanced over at me. The somber look in his eyes gave me a shiver, made me remember he was leaving, and that this evening was the last I'd have with him until he came back home.

But I wasn't about to blurt out how much I'd miss him, any more than he'd be saying that to me. We talked away from how we were feeling, always skipping right over the serious stuff—sort of the way a rock can skip over water, barely touching the surface, then lifting off, light and easy—moving on to joke and wonder about something else.

So while Spit sniffed for field mice in the grass, we went on talking about that box. I asked him again what was inside.

"Who knows? Probably just toenail clippings and bent-up old fishhooks. Maybe a few prune pits . . ."

I gave him a jab in the arm. "Quit teasing," I said. "I want to know."

"Well," he said, looking thoughtful, "I believe I stowed some of Great-aunt Binny's nerve tablets away in there."

He dodged my swing.

"Yes, indeed," he said. "I'm sure I did."

Pretty soon we struck up laughing so hard we nearly fell off the rocks we were sitting on. He jumped up and ran; then we went slipping and sliding down the hill, chasing, laughing, out of breath, Spit running along with us across the back garden, through the gate, bursting into the kitchen, where Mama and the girls were washing dishes.

Mama tried to work up a frown as she reached for a dish towel and walked over to close the door behind us. It was getting dark out. She stopped to switch on the electric lights, then came by and gave Papa a swat with the towel.

He swung around, scooped her up into his arms, and kissed her right there in front of us in the middle of the kitchen.

Helen giggled. I guess five is too young to be embarrassed by something like that. But Alice was nine and just stood across the room fiddling with the knob on the cooler door, looking nervous and uncomfortable. I took time to examine a crack in the ceiling.

When they finally finished, Papa sat down at the table, Mama poured him a cup of hot coffee, and then both girls rushed him like he was a big old piece of apple pie.

"When are you coming home, Papa?" Alice asked.

"In the blink of an eye, little one," he said. "You'll see. I'll be home before Christmas."

"Did you speak to George Morgan?" asked Mama.

Aside from driving stock to market, there are a few other big things to be taken care of when you raise sheep for a living: like lambing, and marking, and of course, shearing. Manpower is important in these matters. That's why all four of our families—the Morgans, the Teales, the Thorntons, and us Farringtons—always did the big work together. For as long as I could remember our daddies had helped each other.

"It's all arranged," Papa said. "He'll be in charge while we're gone. Won't be long. And the Thornton boys will give him a hand. Harley's sixteen now. He knows sheep. I'm trusting they'll do a fine job looking after things."

A fine job? Mr. Morgan surely would, but Luther's big brothers would probably only do a fine job of tormenting the rest of us. I was about to speak my mind on this matter, but just then Helen jumped into Papa's lap and poked him with her finger.

"I have a splinter, Papa. See?" she said.

He looked at it, then motioned to me. "Come here, Joe. Time you took this job over for me." He pulled out that knife of his and put it into my hand. It felt heavy and was still warm from him holding it. "You know how it's done. Be gentle, that's all. Slip the tip of the blade nice and easy, then give a little pull."

"No!" Helen hollered so loud you'd have thought Papa'd just told me to cut out her eyeballs. "You, Papa! I want *you* to do it. Don't let Joe! It'll hurt if he does it!"

Her bottom lip was starting to do that quiver dance it does just before she starts bawling. Mama came over and put her hand on Papa's shoulder. "Maybe *you* ought to do it, Russell. It won't pay to get anyone upset. Not tonight."

Papa sighed; then I sighed to keep him company; then I gave him the knife so he could take out my sister's splinter and keep everyone happy.

I THINK THE DOWNSTAIRS CLOCK chiming five was what woke me, or maybe that first bit of daylight peeking through my curtain. I rolled away from it, listening.

A motor rumbled.

I hauled myself out of bed and hurried to the window, just in time to see Papa and the others drive off in the Thorntons' car. I watched them make their way toward the end of the valley, watched them till they disappeared up over the hill.

I stood there for a long time, staring out at the empty road. I could hear Mama downstairs in the kitchen. The house sounded normal, and felt right for a late-September morning. Cool, airy. I pulled on my clothes and was ready to go down to see her, when I noticed Papa's jackknife on the table by my bed.

Till that split second, I guess I figured life around the house would be pretty much the same as always. He'd just not be there was all. But his knife lying there told me different—told me some of what Papa had not said, some of the serious stuff he'd skipped over last night. Be brave, like him. Be strong. Make him proud. He was trusting me to stand in his stead.

I clearly didn't know if I was ready for that.

CHAPTER 3

READY OR NOT, THERE I WAS—me, Joseph Michael Farrington, all of eleven years old and overnight the boss of the family, charged with looking after my sweet tired mama and my two silly little sisters.

None of my friends had it quite so bad. Sure, Luther's brothers were gone most of the time, boarding at Mrs. Tilley's sister's house over in Maxwell so they could get a high-school education, but they came home some weekends to help Mrs. Thornton and work the sheep. As for Billy, he didn't mind helping his mama—he was used to it, being the only child of Mr. and Mrs. Teale. And of course, Jim Morgan's life didn't change at all—or at least not right away.

I picked up quick on doing the manly chores like the hard lifting around the house. I beat the carpets, turned the mattresses, chopped and stacked the wood. And every day I had to load the kitchen woodbox and prime the pump if that needed to be done; then Mama would send me out to rake leaves, sweep the walk, or ditch the garden. On Tuesdays I'd offer help to Mr. Twining, who delivered the ice. On Saturdays I'd burn the rubbish in the metal drum out back.

It was all hard work, but harder still was seeing that downhearted expression Mama wore for the first few weeks after Papa went away. Sometimes it would be just the two of us reading in the living room at the end of the day, the girls tucked in and asleep upstairs, the house so quiet it made the clock ticking on the mantel sound loud as a hammer. Mama'd get up from her chair, walk to the mantel, and touch the picture of Papa—the one of him in his new uniform. She'd turn to gaze at me, her eyes looking lost and sad, that clock ticking away, and she'd say, "Well, Joe. I guess it's the end of another day."

I'd want to say, "I wonder when Papa will be home," because that's what her eyes were asking. They'd make me start missing Papa so bad I'd have to turn away or leap out of my chair and run to bed. Not one bit brave or manly in the least.

But before we knew it, the weeks rolled away into months, and I got sort of used to living without Papa—used to being the man of the house.

During those months we followed the war-doings on maps cut from the Sunday paper that we stuck up on the kitchen wall with pushpins. We bought Liberty Bonds to support the war effort, donated books for soldiers to read, and twice a week Mama volunteered over at the Red Cross in Maxwell.

But over that time I never tried to take out any splinters for the girls. Once or twice I used Papa's knife to cut twine or slice jerky. And I whittled some. But always in private, not wanting particularly to share the fact that Papa'd given his knife to me. Somehow, I didn't feel like I'd earned it, simply by his going to war. So I mostly just carried it around, letting it be heavy in my pocket as a reminder of him.

IT WAS CLEAR TO ME that Papa'd left me in charge of his knife. And just as clear he'd left Mr. Morgan in charge of the sheep, like he'd said. Unfortunately, I don't think he made that point quite clear enough to Harley Thornton.

From the beginning Harley thought he was a big shot because his daddy'd given him charge of their dogs, Ben and Pete. Ben was a collie, a good reliable sheep dog who'd had lots of practice. Pete was young, but he could round up a wayward ewe fast as lightning. Lots better than our dog, Spit, who wouldn't mind anybody once Papa'd left. So there we were, all of us dependent on Harley and those dogs, while he yelled at them, at his brothers, at us, and sometimes even at Mr. Morgan.

Despite that, we made it through lambing season and on into spring, with Mr. Morgan standing by to even things out in his gentle way, trying to keep the peace.

Sometimes, after the fellows and I'd had supper at Jim's because we'd played late or helped his mama shoo the goats out of her yard, Mr. Morgan would sit down to visit with us on the front steps. He wouldn't say anything at first; he'd just take out his pipe, pull a bag of Prince Albert out of his pants pocket, and shove his pipe full. Believe me, there was no smell in the world sweeter than that pipe tobacco he smoked those evenings on the porch. He'd tamp it down with his thumb, scrape a match along the porch step, then take quick short draws on the pipe till it lit.

He might see something off on the horizon, or get a thought, or have an old horse story to tell, and off he'd go on an easy, rambling journey into another place in his head, his soft words taking us right along.

Maybe Mr. Morgan's gentleness was the reason none of us were too surprised when he didn't go to war. Somehow it was hard to picture him tossing a grenade or stabbing anyone with a bayonet—even a German. Besides, even if some folks said he should have gone off with the rest of them, it was nice just knowing one of our daddies was still around.

PAPA WROTE TO US at least once a week, all about his doings in camp; about how he'd learned to adjust a gas mask and how he'd helped a fellow or two learn to cut barbed wire. The army had him taking French lessons so he'd know how to ask for help if he lost his way in France, and they taught him personal hygiene and proper care of his feet. Not exactly entertaining reading, but it was nice to hear from him just the same.

According to Luther, his daddy mostly wrote about wanting to hurry up and get over to France so he could start killing Germans. Billy's daddy, who'd joined the American Field Service, had already been sent to France to drive an ambulance, so for months, we'd been hearing about the mangled and shot-up and blown-apart bodies Mr. Teale had to pull out of the mud over there. It wasn't that I wanted to hear stuff like that from Papa, but news about something besides his feet might have been nice.

We wrote back to him, of course, the girls in pencil, me in pen and ink, all of us around the big oak table, making sure not to write discouraging things, making sure to tell him that we were all being brave, and that we were getting along fine without him.

Which we were, I guess. Until sometime in April when Papa and Mr. Thornton finally got shipped over to France.

Papa went over with thousands of other soldiers. We were in the thick of the war now, and every day more and more of our fellows were being reported missing or killed.

As it got worse over there in Europe, it got worse over here too. Folks began to worry about spies and foreigners, and more of them spoke up in earnest about hating those Devil Huns. Flags started waving higher, billboards started shouting louder, and folks started pointing out Mr. Morgan as a slacker who was afraid to fight in the war.

Harley picked right up on it, and it didn't take long before he made the big announcement that he wasn't going to let Mr. Morgan take charge of the sheep any longer.

We'd been working up on the hill, all of us helping to string a new line of fence, Harley grumbling whenever Mr. Morgan tried to give him advice. We were almost done, loading up wire and posts and such in the wagon, when Harley marched up and tapped Mr. Morgan on the shoulder.

"Now that school's near finished," he said, "we'll all do just fine running the show without you. Don't want to have to count on a slacker to help us get our work done."

Mr. Morgan didn't protest. He just walked away, stooping to pull a length of grass to chew on, then heading out across the field alone.

That was when I started wondering if we'd make it without Papa. I knew it could only get worse. Once school let out, Luther's brothers would be back on our side of the hill for the whole summer. And we boys knew that the torment they'd dish out would be meaner than ever. What with them feeling so strongly patriotic now, we knew they'd give *all* of us hell every chance they got just because we hung around with Jim.

Summer Soldiers

SUSAN HART LINDQUIST

*During the summer of 1918, eleven-year-old Joe Farrington
learns that those fighting in the trenches of Europe aren't the
only soldiers, and those taking up arms against the Kaiser
aren't the only heroes, in this compassionate tale of small-town
life during the Great War.*

ABOUT THE BOOK

Joe Farrington never imagined that so many fathers in town
would sign up and go to war. Suddenly he finds himself
responsible for doing much of Papa's work on the sheep farm,
and he envies his good friend Jim Morgan, the only kid
whose father didn't enlist. Joe struggles with mixed feelings
about his own father's choice to leave, as well as Mr. Morgan's
choice to stay home, and questions his closest friendships.

When Mr. Morgan sacrifices his own life to save tethered
horses from a shipwreck, Joe is strengthened by his family
and friendships. He comes to terms with Mr. Morgan's death
and his own father's missing-in-action status as he discovers
that true courage comes from doing what you think is right . . .
no matter what the cost.

PRE-READING ACTIVITY

Using library and Internet resources, assist students in understanding the political context of World War I and the causes of the later involvement by the United States. Highlight the discussion with war terms and practices that students will encounter while reading the novel, such as *Hooverizing* (p. 39), *Allied trenches* (p. 42), *Four-Minute Men* (p. 44), and *U-boat* (p. 48).

THEMATIC CONNECTIONS

∾ **Courage and Honor**—Because of Mr. Morgan's heroic sacrifice at the novel's end, Joe and others are forced to rethink conventional ideas of courage and cowardice. After defining and giving examples of each of these terms, ask students their views of Mr. Morgan's nature, choices, and actions and the townspeople's reactions to them. Have students search the novel for examples of different kinds of courage and cowardice.

∾ **Friendship**—Ask students to describe each of the four personalities in Joe's Hobby Horse Gang. What makes their friendships so strong? How are they tested? What insights do they gain into each other as the events of this turbulent summer unfold? Ask students to reflect on important friendships of their own, and the ways in which their friendships enrich their lives.

ⵁ **Patriotism**—Have your students compare the 1918 Fourth of July festivities in Joe's hometown with those today. Who are the patriots honored? How are they honored? Why? Ask students to define what patriotism means to Joe, the Thornton boys, Mr. Morgan, and other townspeople. Have students form their own definitions of patriotism. Discuss different ways men and women may serve their country, and the values society seems to place on each.

ⵁ **Making Choices**—When Joe goes to Mama with his troubles, she tells him, "Do whatever you think is right." However, Joe isn't sure he knows what's right. Was it right for Papa to leave his family? For the townspeople to drive out Karl Bauer and shun the Morgans? Should Joe sever ties with his best friend? Joe's dilemmas lead students to understand that doing what's right sometimes comes with great risk and that we all need to make personal, often unpopular choices.

ⵁ **Keepsakes**—After Papa is listed as missing in action, Joe searches obsessively for an old cookie tin in which Papa kept special things. What does Joe expect to find in this box? Why is it so important? Why are the secret things hidden at the Pepperwood Grove so important? Have your students create keepsake boxes of their own.

INTERDISCIPLINARY CONNECTIONS

Language Arts—Have your students put themselves in Joe's shoes, allowing them to express in a letter to Papa what they see as Joe's true feelings and his confusion about the war, Papa's absence, and things happening at home. Encourage them to ask questions that they think Joe would ask if given the opportunity.

After identifying two of Aunt Binny's favorite poets (Christina Rossetti and Henry Wadsworth Longfellow) and another of the period (Joyce Kilmer), direct students to library and Internet resources to research a prominent poet and choose a poem for recitation. Have them highlight major points of interest in written biographical summaries and share both poem and biography with classmates.

Science—Daylight saving time was a new idea during the period when *Summer Soldiers* takes place. Using library and Internet resources, have your students define daylight saving time (DST) and standard time. Discuss the present-day practice of moving clocks ahead one hour in the spring and back one hour in the fall. Identify the origins of DST and the reasons that various countries do or do not participate in it. Ask students which time they prefer and why.

Geography—Joe and his friends often refer to the European area in which their fathers are fighting as no-man's- land. Using library or Internet map resources, help students gain a clearer geographic sense of the war fronts and other important WWI sites.

Social Studies—Throughout the novel, Joe, his family, and his friends comment on important men and women of the period, including Woodrow Wilson, General Pershing, Kaiser Wilhelm, Mata Hari, Major Billy Bishop, and Ty Cobb. Using library and Internet resources, have your students work in pairs to research these historical figures. Then have the pairs of students conduct mock interviews in front of the class.

Summer soldiers is the term given to those Americans, like Joe's father, who came late to the war. How might this term also apply to Joe, his friends, and their families, whose lives were touched by the Great War and who were fighting battles of a different kind?

VOCABULARY/USE OF LANGUAGE

Throughout the novel, descriptive similes such as "clean and fresh as a meadow" (p. 7) and "like a kettle ready to start off whistling" (p. 137) convey concrete images of time and place. Have students search the text for other such descriptors, discussing how each embellishes the novel's setting.

Lily's Crossing
Patricia Reilly Giff
- World War II
- Friendship

Grades 4–7 / 0-440-41453-9

Soldier's Heart
Gary Paulsen
- The Civil War
- Courage
- Patriotism

Grades 7 up / 0-440-22838-7

The War in Georgia
Jerrie Oughton
- World War II
- Family

Grades 7 up / 0-440-22752-6

Teaching ideas prepared by Rosemary B. Stimola, Ph.D., professor of children's literature at the City University of New York and educational consultant

ABOUT THE AUTHOR

Susan Hart Lindquist has always lived in California, where the countryside has been the setting for many of her stories, including *Summer Soldiers*. Although Ms. Lindquist loves the wilderness and wide-open spaces, she also enjoys the hustle and bustle of city living. Filled with people, noise, and good food and music, cities often offer her an experience similar to that of being in the countryside—as if she belongs to something much bigger and more important than herself.

Photo credit: Paul Lindquist

When she was a child, everything about school was difficult for Ms. Lindquist. Besides being a reluctant reader, she preferred to daydream and often forgot to do her homework—two bad habits which, ironically, helped her develop skills that came in handy when she began writing fiction. Her daydreaming gave her the opportunity to practice using her imagination and inventing excuses (really good stories) to explain why her homework wasn't done!

Ms. Lindquist earned a bachelor's degree from the University of California, Santa Barbara, and is a writing instructor and poet as well as the author of two previous children's novels, including *Wander*. She lives in Walnut Creek with her husband, Paul, their children, Charlie, Madeline, and Sam, and their dog, Jack.

THREE AGAINST THE TIDE

D. Anne Love

A Yearling Book

For Regina Griffin
who sees angels in the marble

Contents

NB: Page numbers correspond to actual paperback book, not this teacher's edition.

Chapter One

The Visitor

If you ask people in Charleston when the war began, they will tell you about a springtime morning when ladies cheered from rooftops and cannon fire thundered. For me it began on a Sunday in late October, when everything around me—the house, the fields, the patient river—slept peacefully in a golden haze.

Until an unexpected visitor broke the stillness of that afternoon, Terrapin Island had seemed a quiet, separate kingdom, and the cruel crusade that had begun six months before nothing more than a fleeting cloud on the distant horizon.

Papa was in his study reading. Neddie and Sammy were fishing in the tidal creek that curled through the woods behind our house. From my window I could see their heads bobbing in the tall grasses, Neddie's dark as a raven's wing, Sammy's the brownish gold of a rice field at harvest-time.

Sammy's laughter rang through the trees. I put down

my pen. I dearly missed fishing with my brothers, but my twelfth birthday had passed and Papa said it was time to learn to be a lady. That meant wearing miles of petticoats and scratchy lace collars. It meant writing in a journal every day, whether or not I had anything to say. It seemed a tragic waste of a perfect afternoon to be sitting alone writing out the particulars of my day, especially when the fish were biting. But Papa was determined to bring me up in a manner befitting a girl of my station, and I was determined to please Papa.

"Susanna! Papa! Somebody's coming!" That was Neddie.

Happy for any reason to abandon my journal, I stepped onto the second-floor piazza that wrapped around our house. From there I could see our long avenue, shaded with oak trees, and beyond it the silvery gleam of the river. A stranger on a black horse charged onto the road, raising a cloud of dust in his wake.

I went downstairs to the parlor, wondering who could be calling on us so soon. We had returned to Terrapin Island from our house in town on Tuesday last and weren't yet ready to receive visitors.

Papa came out of his study carrying his book, his spectacles perched on the end of his nose. "Susanna, what's Neddie yelling about?"

Before I could answer, Neddie burst through the door, Sammy at his heels. "Papa! There's a man coming. He's a general or something."

"He'd better not be a Yankee general," Sammy said. "I'll

shoot him like this." Lifting both his arms, he pretended to aim a musket. "Pow! Right between the eyes!"

"Samuel," Papa said, frowning, "you must never speak about a man's life that way. This war is a terrible thing. Now go tell Sipsy to set another place. We have a guest."

The rider galloped into the yard and dismounted. Joseph, one of our grooms, came to lead the horse away. Brushing the dust from his uniform, the rider said, "Are you Doc Simons?"

"I am. And who are you, sir?"

"Captain Jonas Trimble's the name. From Colonel Martin's cavalry."

"What brings you to Oakwood, Captain Trimble?" Papa rested one hand on my shoulder, the other on Neddie's.

"A message from General Lee himself." Then he said, "But it ain't something that ought to be discussed in front of children."

"Can it wait a bit?" Papa said pleasantly. "The next ferry isn't for a couple of hours yet, and we're just about to have our dinner. Will you join us?"

"Oh, I wouldn't want to put you to any trouble."

"Not at all," Papa said. "We'd be honored."

For Papa, hospitality was as important as religion.

"Well, if you're sure," Captain Trimble said. "I could use a hot meal, and that's the honest truth. Living on corn dodgers is no life for anybody, I can tell you that."

Papa and I led the way to the dining room. Sipsy, our cook, brought out soup and corn bread and plates of corn and ham and potatoes. She set a basket of fruit and a cake with thick white icing in the middle of the table.

While we ate, Captain Trimble told us how he hoped to have a plantation as fine as Oakwood someday. "How many acres you got here? If you don't mind my asking."

Neddie's eyes went wide. Even he understood what an impolite question it was. But we shouldn't have been surprised. Since the beginning of the war, all manner of men had rushed to join the army. Not all of them were gentlemen. Yet Papa was not one to embarrass a guest. "Almost two thousand," he answered, picking up his coffee cup. "Mostly in rice and cotton. And we have cattle."

"Two thousand acres! It must take a trainload of workers to keep it going."

"Indeed," Papa said. "That's why our labor supply must be preserved. The Northerners don't understand how important it is for us."

"Now there's a truth! They preach to us that slavery is wrong, but they wouldn't last ten minutes without our rice and cotton."

Just then Sipsy glided in, carrying the milk pitcher and my mother's silver coffeepot on a tray. She poured more coffee for Papa and our visitor and more milk for the boys and me.

Captain Trimble said to Papa, "Where's your missus today? If you don't mind my asking."

From across the table Neddie stared at me as if to say, "Another impossibly rude question!"

Papa's gaze slid to the portrait of our mother that hung

above the fireplace. "We lost her four years ago last February. I don't know how I'd have managed all this time without Susanna."

"Fine-looking woman. What happened to her?"

Sammy spoke up. "She died when the twins were born. They died, too."

At least Captain Trimble had the grace to look embarrassed. He cleared his throat and said to me, "Why, you ain't no bigger than a minute. How old are you?"

As if my age were any of his concern! But I said, "Almost thirteen."

"And wise beyond her years," Papa said.

"That must be some job," Captain Trimble said. "Taking care of this big house and two young boys to boot."

"I'm not young," Neddie declared. "I'm eleven. I don't need anyone to take care of me."

"Me neither," Sammy said. "I'm rough and tough and strong as an ox."

Captain Trimble laughed. "You look pretty strong, all right."

After we finished our cake, Neddie put down his fork and said, "Captain, what does General Lee want with our papa?"

Leaning back in his chair, the captain said to Papa, "May I talk with them present?"

"Go ahead."

"Well then. General Lee is on his way to Charleston," the captain began, "to organize our troops, along with the men from Georgia and Florida."

"Just wait till those Yankees tangle with us," Sammy said. "We'll have them running lickety-split."

"Sammy, do you wish to be excused?" Papa asked quietly.

Captain Trimble continued. "The Confederate Congress has been investigating our military hospitals. Doc, they're a real mess. Fevers, lice, and—"

"I understand," Papa put in quickly. "Go on."

"Well then. Ever since Manassas, the hospitals have been overcrowded. The men . . ." His voice died away and he glanced at me. "This ain't fit for a girl to hear."

"Susanna?" Papa queried.

"I want to stay."

"It's a sight to make a grown man cry," the captain continued. "They lie there burning with fever and all twisted up with pain. There's hardly any medicine."

"I've heard there's not even quinine," Papa said, "except what the blockade runners smuggle in."

"It's the truth. The doctors can't get chloroform, neither. They're taking off arms and legs without anything stronger than a sip of whiskey to dull the pain."

A look that was part pain, part anger flickered on Papa's face. "That's barbaric! I can't believe the Yankee people are so cruel they won't even let medical supplies through."

Sammy set his empty glass on the table. "*I* can believe it. I heard that when Yankees get really old, their children kill them and eat them."

Neddie snickered. I almost laughed, too, till I saw Papa's scowl. "You're excused, Samuel," he said.

"Yes sir." Leaving his napkin on his chair, he plodded up the stairs. Poor Sammy. He could get into more mischief in one day than Neddie or I could manage in an entire month.

"Forgive me, Captain," Papa said. "Please go on."

"General Lee wants to know if you'll meet him in Charleston the day after tomorrow to plan an inspection of the hospitals. To see if you have any ideas on how to straighten this mess out."

Neddie and I exchanged hasty glances across the table. Surely with a war on, Papa wouldn't leave us. Even if General Lee wanted him. For a moment the only sounds were the ticking of the mantel clock and the whispering of the sea in the tidal creek.

Papa stroked his beard. "When I think of all those young boys lying wounded, some not much older than Neddie, how can I refuse?"

"Then you'll come?" Captain Trimble looked relieved.

"Yes," Papa said. "I will."

It was hard to believe Papa would make such an important decision without consulting us, but there it was.

Papa said, "Allow me to speak to my overseer first and arrange for the care of my children. Tell the general I'll meet him in the city."

"I'll tell him." The captain turned to me. "Appreciate the meal, miss. You'll make a fine plantation mistress someday."

"Oh no." My words tumbled out. "I'm going to be a doctor."

"Is that so? I don't reckon I ever heard of a female doctor."

"Where have you been?" Papa asked. "Elizabeth Blackwell got her medical degree back in 'forty-nine." He put his arm around my shoulder. "Susanna's made rounds with me since she was nine years old. She'll make a fine doctor someday."

Papa's words gladdened my heart. Riding on rounds with him, learning how to mix medicines and heal the sick, was the one thing that made his efforts to turn me into a lady bearable.

"If you say so," the captain said. "But all that book learning is wasted on a girl." He laughed, a most disagreeable sound. "You're young yet. You'll change your mind when some young gentleman takes a fancy to you."

"No, I won't."

"Once Susanna sets her mind to something, she's like a dog on a bone," Papa said. "Come, Captain, I'll see you out."

They went out onto the porch, still talking, their voices low. Neddie sat down on the bottom stair and rested his chin in his hands. "Will Papa send the overseer's wife to stay with us?"

"I don't see how, Neddie. She has four children of her own to look after."

"Maybe Mrs. Miles then."

"Maybe."

"That wouldn't be so bad. Sammy would be happy. He'd have Stephen for a playmate."

"But then it would be lonely for you." I sat on the stair beside him. "Don't you ever wish for a best friend?"

"Don't need one," Neddie said. "I've got you."

I wanted to hug him, but lately he'd acted embarrassed by even the smallest show of affection. So I gave his shoulder a good wallop instead.

He stood up. "Looks like Papa and that captain are going to talk all night. Might as well fetch Sammy and go fishing."

The boys left, and after a while Papa summoned me to the porch.

The tide was out. The damp, fishy breath of the mud-flats hung in the air.

Papa settled into his rocking chair and lit his pipe. I leaned against the porch railing. "Is that horrid man gone?"

"He is." Gray smoke curled over his head. "I don't think he quite knew what to make of you."

"I'm sorry, Papa. I didn't mean to be rude, but I couldn't help it."

"He had it coming," Papa said. "However, for your own sake, my dear, I hope you'll learn to be more tactful. A true lady tempers her speech. She can't always say exactly what's on her mind." He put down his pipe. "Where are the boys?"

"Gone fishing."

"Good. I want to speak with you privately."

Something in his voice made my heart skip. "What is it?"

"There's more to General Lee's request than you know," he began. "It seems there's a fleet of Yankee ships heading this way. Close to fifty in all, Captain Trimble says. Most of them are armed."

"But they wouldn't come to Terrapin Island, would they?"

"They blame South Carolina for starting the war. According to the captain, there are thousands of Yankee soldiers on their way here, too. There's some talk they may try to take Port Royal."

"But that's only forty miles from here!"

His expression was troubled. "That would be the worst possible thing, Susanna. If they capture Port Royal, they could reach Oakwood in two days. Three at the most. We'd be trapped."

"But Papa, what can *you* do about it?"

"The general needs someone who can find out what the Yankees are planning without making them suspicious. By visiting our hospitals, I can travel around, talk to soldiers, listen for information about the Yankees. If I discover anything useful, I'll pass it on to General Lee."

At first it was difficult to fathom his meaning. When at last I did, I could scarcely believe it. Our papa, a Confederate spy.

Chapter Two

The Secret

I stared at Papa in the darkness. The moon came up, painting the tops of the water oaks with a silver light.

"It will be dangerous," he said quietly. "But I have no choice. This war is more than a fight over slavery. Oakwood has been in our family for over a hundred years. I must do whatever I can to protect it."

Perhaps I should have felt proud of Papa, but I was frightened and disappointed that he'd agreed to such a dangerous plan without even talking it over with me. What would become of the boys and me if he was captured or killed?

Extracting an envelope from his pocket, Papa went on. "This is for your cousin Hettie down in Savannah. If anything should happen, if I should be delayed for a long time, find Captain Trimble and give him this letter. He'll see that she comes to take care of you."

The mere thought of Cousin Hettie filled me with dismay. She was so ill-tempered I would rather live with strangers than with her. All the same, I tucked the letter into my pocket.

The boys were returning from the creek. Papa knocked the ashes from his pipe. "I know it's a terrible burden, but you must keep this a secret. The fewer people who know about it, the safer I'll be. Do you understand?"

"Yes, Papa." Hot tears flooded my eyes.

"That's my girl." He stood up and his chair squeaked. "It's only for a short while. Try not to worry."

Sammy and Neddie clattered up the steps. "Look what I brought for you, Papa," Neddie said, holding up his string of fish. "Three bream."

"My favorite!" Papa clapped Neddie on the shoulder. "Thank you, son."

Then Neddie turned to me, his mouth tilted up into a smile. Putting one leg out, he bowed low, like a prince bowing to a queen. "And for you, fair princess, the most beautiful flowers of the field." He handed me a bouquet of cattails, sea oats, and purple asters.

A hard lump settled in my throat. Truth to tell, I was plain as a mud fence. Nobody would ever mistake me for a fair princess. But Neddie was a born gentleman. He could make even a troll feel beautiful.

Sammy tugged at my sleeve. "What's wrong with you?"

"Nothing. I'm perfectly fine."

"Are not," he said. "You're crying 'cause you don't want Papa to go."

"Of course I don't, you little goose."

"I'll bet General Lee makes Papa a general, too,"

Sammy said. "I'll bet Papa comes back with ten thousand medals and a fine white horse. I'll bet he kills a million Yankees."

"I'm not going to kill anyone," Papa told him. "I'm going to visit the hospitals and then come home. And when I get back, we'll make our Christmas plans."

"Oh, good!" Sammy crowed. "I want a Springfield rifled musket that shoots real ammunition."

"You won't be getting a musket," Papa informed him. "Not this year, anyway."

Sammy stared at Papa as if he couldn't quite believe his ears. "Are you sure?"

"Certain." He lifted Sammy up until their eyes were level. "I'm counting on you to obey Susanna while I'm away. Find some useful way to occupy your time, and do your best to keep out of mischief, all right, Sam?"

Sammy wrapped his arms around Papa's neck. "Yes sir. I know a million ways to keep busy."

Papa chuckled. "That's what worries me."

We went inside. Stopping at his study, Papa said to me, "If you like, you may go with me to the overseer's in the morning. I should check on his daughter's foot before I leave. That was a nasty gash she got last week."

"Yes, Papa." It was his way of making up, but it didn't make me feel the least bit better. Inside my head questions rattled around like marbles in a jar. Who would look after us while Papa was away? Sipsy and Kit? That seemed unlikely. After all, we were accustomed to telling the servants what to do, not the other way around. And suppose something dreadful happened to Papa. What would we do then?

I slept fitfully, waking at the slightest sounds. In the morning, Papa knocked on my door. "Susanna? Wake up."

The floor was cold beneath my feet. I dressed hurriedly and met Papa in the dining room. After breakfast, we went out to our buggy.

Elias was waiting in the shade of the trees. Papa favored him above all our other servants. He was strong and intelligent and could build and fix almost anything. He always carried his tools in a wooden box balanced on his shoulder.

"Elias!" Papa set his medical bag on the porch and shaded his eyes. "What brings you here?"

Elias set his toolbox down. "Mr. Barnes sent me to fix the smokehouse roof. But the fence down by the cow pasture is a-falling down. One good kick and all your cows be a-running six ways to Sunday."

"I see," Papa replied. "This sudden interest in the fence—it wouldn't have anything to do with the fact that it's cooler down by the river than up on the roof, would it?"

"Oh, no sir!" Elias shook his head. "Seem like them cattle be most valuable to you. Seem like you wouldn't want them lost in the woods. Figure on a-fixing that fence and saving you a heap of trouble."

"Did you mention this to Mr. Barnes?" Papa inquired.

Elias stared at his feet. "You know he all full of hisself. A-hollering and a-carrying on like this whole plantation his. He don't like nobody telling him nothing. Figure I best come to you."

Papa said, "I do appreciate it, Elias. But you must follow the overseer's orders. Suppose the hands suddenly began questioning which crops to harvest. Can you see how that could cause trouble?"

Stung by Papa's rebuke, Elias stared past us as if we'd suddenly ceased to exist.

"You go on now,'" Papa instructed. "Get started on the smokehouse. I'll speak to Barnes about the fence."

Muttering to himself, Elias picked up his tools and walked off. We settled into the buggy. Joseph handed Papa the reins and we curved along the road, past the fields toward the overseer's house.

Papa said, "After you went to bed last night, I rode over to Summerhill to see Mrs. Miles. You and the boys will stay there with her till I come back."

"What about Mr. Miles? Everyone says he's acting strangely these days."

"He seemed all right to me," Papa said. "A bit tired perhaps, but he's not slept well since Darcy left. It must be heartbreaking to see your oldest boy going off to war."

As we drove into the overseer's yard, the chickens squawked and flapped and ran under the porch. Mr. Barnes was in the side yard, chopping firewood. He drove his ax into his chopping block, wiped his hands on his trousers, and came to meet us.

"I apologize for the early hour," Papa said to him. "I have business in the city. Thought we'd check on Lucy's foot before I go."

"Come on in then, if you're a mind to."

We went inside. While Papa removed Lucy's bandage, I opened his medicine bag and took out the salve. But my thoughts returned to poor Mr. Miles. Papa always insists a lady never credits gossip, but everyone on Terrapin Island said Mr. Miles hadn't been himself after Darcy joined the Confederates. People said he'd taken to his bed with his whiskey bottle and lost all interest in his plantation. Even if every word of it was true, there was nothing I could do. Papa had given his word to General Lee.

After Papa put a clean bandage on Lucy's foot, we went outside. Papa said to the overseer, "When will you start the rice harvest?"

"Tomorrow, if there's no rain. Cotton'll be ready this week, too."

"How are the field hands? Sipsy said a few were sick last week."

"You know how they are. Always complaining about something. To hear them talk, you'd think they were never well. Rosie and Peggy both had babies last week. They're useless right now, and here we sit on the biggest cotton crop in years." He swatted at a water bug buzzing around his face. "I can't get blood from a turnip. We need more workers. Plain and simple."

Papa looked thoughtful. "Cotton ought to top sixty cents a pound this year, more for the best quality. Go see John Thomas over on St. Helena. He owes me a favor. Perhaps he'll rent us some workers."

A frightened look came into the overseer's eyes. "If you ask me, putting a bunch of slaves in a boat is just courting trouble."

"Ask Thomas to send his overseer back with you," Papa advised. "Oh. I almost forgot. Elias came by this morning. Says the fence in the cow pasture is coming down."

"Oh, he did, did he?" Mr. Barnes scratched his arm. "That's one slave that's getting way too big for his britches, to my way of thinking. You'll have trouble with that one before it's all over. Mark my words."

Papa went on as if he hadn't heard. "Take a look at it, will you? And the floodgate in the number eight field is broken, too. Send Elias on over there to fix it."

The overseer's mouth puckered as if he'd just bitten into a green persimmon. "What's the hurry? Won't be no more rice planting till next spring."

"Nevertheless, I'd rather you saw to it now," Papa returned. "Once planting season rolls around again, you'll be too busy. It shouldn't take too long. Elias is handy with tools."

"I've seen better. And I don't aim to put up with him going to you behind my back. You can't expect me to keep these people in line if they know they can run to you for every little thing."

"Do the best you can, Barnes." Papa handed me into the buggy and set his bag inside. "I'll expect a full accounting when I return."

He climbed in, flicked the reins, and we drove out of the yard.

"Why do you keep Mr. Barnes on, Papa? He's always so unpleasant."

"That he is," Papa agreed. "I suppose he's never gotten over losing his own farm. It must sorely try his soul to have to work for me. But with so many men joining the army, I'm lucky to have him. If this war goes on very long, there won't be anyone left to run Oakwood."

We drove on through the cool morning, Papa's little mare stepping smartly along the road. Through the trees, the sun gleamed bright as a gold coin, and the fallen leaves danced in the wind. Usually such an outing with Papa was a happy event, but now that he was going away, sadness pushed the joy from my heart.

Too soon, we were home. Papa's horse was waiting in the shade. Handing the buggy over to Joseph, he picked up his lumpy saddlebags and swung into his saddle.

"No tears, now," he said, smiling down at me. "These are troublesome times, and we all must be brave."

I didn't feel brave. I wanted to jump up beside him, put my arms around him, and hold on for dear life.

"Mrs. Miles will call for you around noon." Papa shifted his weight. The leather creaked. "See that the boys mind their manners, Susanna. And take care of Oakwood. I'm counting on you."

"Yes, Papa. Please be careful, and come back soon."

"I shouldn't be gone more than a couple of weeks. With Mrs. Miles to keep you company, it won't seem like such a long time. Goodbye, my dear. Kiss the boys for me. It's so early, I didn't want to wake them." He turned his horse and was gone.

I went inside. Sammy hurtled along the upstairs hallway, slid down the banister feetfirst, and landed with a thud. "Has Papa left yet?"

"Yes."

"Drat! I wanted to give him my rabbit's foot for good luck."

From his place on the stairs, Neddie winked at me. "You don't really believe in that hocus-pocus, do you, Sammy?"

"The Negroes keep all kinds of things for good luck, even dried-up lizards and snake skins," Sammy said. "I don't reckon a rabbit's foot would hurt. Would it, Susanna?"

"I suppose not. Go upstairs and pack your things now. We're going to stay with Mrs. Miles at Summerhill."

On the porch, we waited for Mrs. Miles's carriage. Twelve o'clock came. Then one o'clock.

"Are you sure she's coming today?" Neddie asked.

"I'm sure." But I worried that she'd forgotten us after all.

Then, up the river road came a lone rider on a gray horse. Sammy jumped up. "That can't be her! Unless we're all going to Summerhill on one old horse."

Neddie squinted into the sun. "I think it's Harrison. Mrs. Miles always makes him wear that black suit."

Harrison rode into the yard. "Miss Susanna? Mrs. Miles say tell you she's powerful sorry, but you can't stay at Summerhill after all."

"What? Why not?"

"Mr. Miles, he feeling most raggedy this morning, and Mrs. Miles say it's more than she can do to take care of the house and Master Stephen and the baby, and all of you, too."

"But she promised Papa!"

"Yessum. She say don't worry none. She a-coming by to visit you next week."

"Next week? What are we supposed to do till then? What if the Yankees—"

Neddie whirled around. "Yankees?"

"It's nothing, Neddie. I was just thinking out loud."

"Well," Harrison said. "I got to go. Mrs. Miles say if I ain't back in one hour, she set the dogs on my trail."

I watched him ride away. I was furious with Mrs. Miles. The prospect of staying at Oakwood alone made me sick with worry. I knew how to clean and dress a wound and how to mix medicines for a fever, but I'd never been in charge of an entire plantation.

Neddie's arm came around my shoulders. "Never mind. We don't need her. We don't need anybody. We can manage just fine. You and me."

THREE AGAINST THE TIDE

D. Anne Love

Three children, accustomed to a privileged life on a Southern plantation, embark on a dangerous journey to locate their father when he is away inspecting Confederate hospitals during the Civil War.

IN THE CLASSROOM

In the author's note, D. Anne Love explains that the setting and characters in *Three Against the Tide* are imaginary, but the historical facts about the Civil War and the invasion of Port Royal in Charleston, South Carolina, are based on actual events. For this reason, this is an excellent novel to use with social studies classes for a study of the Civil War.

Themes of *courage, survival, fear, betrayal, friendship,* and *changes* offer students the opportunity to examine the effect of war on families and the insecurity of facing a new life. In addition, this guide provides activities that link the language arts, social studies, science, music, and art.

PRE-READING ACTIVITY

Discuss with your class the term *historical fiction* and why this book is categorized as such. Display a map of the Confederate states, then locate Port Royal in Charleston, South Carolina. Define the word *secession* and discuss the many reasons why the Southern states voted to secede from the Union. Ask students to find out about the event in South Carolina that officially began the Civil War.

THEMATIC CONNECTIONS

COURAGE—When the Simonses' house burns, Susanna says, "We will not feel sorry for ourselves" (p. 112). How does this statement display courage? How does Susanna instill courage in her siblings? When the children return from their dangerous journey, Miss Hastings says, "Somehow, I think it had more to do with common sense and uncommon courage" (p. 157). Explain what she means by "uncommon courage."

FEAR—Susanna says, "Despite all my book learning, I knew little that was useful in real life" (p. 59). Discuss how Susanna's lack of real life experience contributes to her fears. How does Susanna react when she discovers that her father is spying? How do her fears give her the courage to keep her family together and to search for her father?

ॐ **BETRAYAL**—The children discover that Elias has stolen their mother's silver sugar bowl. Explain Elias's reasoning when he says, "But that bowl a mighty small payment for a whole lifetime a-working on your pappy's plantation" (p. 55). Discuss why Susanna gives the bowl to Elias. Engage the class in a discussion about why Susanna did not betray Elias.

ॐ **FRIENDSHIP**—Describe Mrs. Miles from Susanna's point of view (p. 73). How does Miss Hastings offer help? How does Mr. Miller show his support? When Susanna asks Neddie if he ever wishes for a friend, he replies, "Don't need one. I've got you" (p. 9). Discuss the relationship among the three Simons siblings. How is their relationship like a friendship?

ॐ **CHANGES**—At the end of the novel, Susanna says, "Because of the war, we were changed forever. We could never go back to the way it was before" (p. 158). To what changes is Susanna referring? How does the war change her personally? How did the war change the South forever?

ॐ **CAREERS**—Susanna had high hopes of becoming a doctor, but Captain Timble laughed at the idea. Why was this notion thought ridiculous in 1861? What type of "work" did women do back then? How is that different from today?

INTERDISCIPLINARY CONNECTIONS

LANGUAGE ARTS—Ask students to write a journal entry that Susanna might have written on the day when she and her brothers evacuated Oakwood Plantation on Terrapin Island.

D. Anne Love uses imagery to illuminate the text. For example, "Night on the river was beautiful and mysterious" (p. 51). Ask students to locate other examples of imagery in the novel. How do Love's words paint a picture in the reader's mind?

SOCIAL STUDIES—The novel takes place at the beginning of the Civil War. Ask students to discuss the differences between a battle, a campaign, and a raid. Divide the class into small groups and ask each group to research one of the following Civil War events and give a short presentation to the class: the Battle of Bull Run, the Battle of Shiloh, the Battle of New Orleans, the Burning of Atlanta, the Andrews Raid, the Seven Days Campaign, the Vicksburg Campaign, the Chattanooga Campaign, and the Battle of Gettysburg.

Slave labor was important in the American South because plantation owners needed people to work in the fields. Ask students to find out about the living and working conditions of migrant workers today and list the differences between slave labor and migrant labor.

SCIENCE—What medicines does Susanna use to treat Neddie's illness? Have students research other medicines, herbs, and plants used to treat various medical problems during the 1800s. Then have them construct a simple medical guide for families that Dr. Simons might have written, explaining different medicines and their uses.

Use examples from the book (pp. 6–7) to discuss the conditions in army hospitals during wartime. How did Susanna help lift the spirits of the wounded soldiers? How did her visit affect her decision to become a doctor?

MUSIC—On February 18, 1861, Jefferson Davis became president of the Confederate States, and the song "Dixie" was played at his inauguration. Ask students to research the origin of the song. Though it is widely associated with the American South, discuss why "Dixie" is historically important to all of America.

A Dangerous Promise
0-440-21965-5
Keeping Secrets
0-440-21992-2
Joan Lowery Nixon
- Challenges
- Family and Relationships
- Making Choices
Grades 5–7

The Last Silk Dress
Ann Rinaldi
- Courage
- Challenges
Grades 5–7 / 0-553-28315-4

Nightjohn
Gary Paulsen
- Survival
- Prejudice
Grades 7 up / 0-440-21936-1

With Every Drop of Blood: A Novel of the Civil War
James Lincoln Collier and Christopher Collier
- Making Choices
- Prejudice
Grades 5 up / 0-440-21983-3

Prepared by Pat Scales, Director of Library Services,
South Carolina Governor's School for the Arts and
Humanities, Greenville

"Readers often ask which parts of a story are fiction and which are true. Terrapin Island and Oakwood Plantation are fictional, but they are based upon actual places in the South Carolina low country. Except for General Lee, all the characters are fictional as well. I was inspired to create the character of Susanna Simons after reading about the real-life Eliza Lucas, who, in 1739, was left in charge of three South Carolina plantations at age fifteen while her father was away serving in the British army.

"While the setting and characters are imaginary, the invasion by federal troops at Port Royal and the great fire that destroyed much of Charleston actually happened much as I've described them. As terrible as these events were, they were only the beginning of trouble. . . .

"If you visit the Sea Islands today, stand beneath the ancient trees and listen with your heart. There, amid the silent ruins of a time long past, perhaps you will hear the voices of children from long ago rising up like mist on the river, borne homeward on the evening tide."

—from the author's note, *Three Against the Tide*

D. Anne Love's most recent novel is *Three Against the Tide*. She is also the author of *Bess's Log Cabin Quilt* and *Dakota Spring*, both set on the American frontier, as well as *My Lone Star Summer*. Ms. Love enjoys researching and writing historical fiction. Born and raised in Texas, she now lives in Iowa, where she is a program consultant for an educational agency.

PRAISE FOR

A Letter to Mrs. Roosevelt

"This historical novel is successful in conveying the climate of the times. . . . Margo emerges as an admirable heroine whose actions reveal a generous heart and determination to help her family hold on to their home."

—*Publishers Weekly*

"Readers will find amiable characters here, as well as a clear picture of the time's anxieties and hardships."

—*Kirkus Reviews*

"Based on a true family story, this novel . . . creates a strong sense of place and time, when the Depression was felt up to the front porch of a loving family home."

—*Booklist*

Honors for *A Letter to Mrs. Roosevelt*

A *Booklist* Top 10 First Novels for Youth

Winner of the Marguerite de Angeli Prize

A Letter to Mrs. Roosevelt

C. COCO DE YOUNG

A Yearling Book

Published by
Dell Yearling
an imprint of
Random House Children's Books
a division of Random House, Inc.
1540 Broadway
New York, New York 10036

To order classroom sets of
A Letter to Mrs. Roosevelt (ISBN 0-440-41529-2) in paperback,
please contact your local distributor or bookstore.

Promotional copy—not for sale

Visit us on the Web! www.randomhouse.com/kids

**Educators and librarians, for a variety of teaching tools, visit us at
www.randomhouse.com/teachers**

ISBN 0-440-41529-2

Reprinted by arrangement with Delacorte Press

Printed in the United States of America

August 2000

OPM

In loving memory of my grandparents,
Mike and Carmela Coco
and
Giuseppe and Giuseppina Camuti

To my beloved parents, the believers,
Carmel and Mary Kay (Camuti) Coco

For my dream keepers,
Don, Bryan, CaraMarie, Lauren, and Marisa

Chapter 1

~

THE SHOOTING STAR
JOHNSTOWN, PENNSYLVANIA

I never used to pay much attention to the dark. Well, except for the nights when I sat on our front-porch swing, counting the stars and waiting. I would find a patch of stars caught between the rooftops across the street and swing and count, and count and wait.

One night my best friend's mother called to me from her porch next door, "Margo, go inside. It's raining. There are no stars for you to count."

"Thank you, Mrs. Meglio, but I can still see the stars from last night," I called back. I didn't tell her that my eyes were closed tight and I was trying to remember them.

Nighttime was my friend back then, keeping me company while I waited for the trolley car to bring Mama and Papa home. I could hear the clatter as it crossed over the First Street Bridge and turned right onto Maple Avenue. Papa would climb down the steps, then hold out his hand to Mama. I could tell right then if Charlie—he's my little brother—had had a good day or bad.

Charlie had been kicked in the knee when he'd tried to break up a fight between two boys during a game of kickball. He'd convinced Mama and Papa that it was an accident, but I was not so sure. I can remember hearing Charlie groan during the night. I went in to check him, but he was sound asleep. The next morning Charlie's knee looked like a balloon. He stayed in bed all day. It didn't help. When the doctor visited that evening he told Papa to get Charlie to the hospital immediately. The infection in Charlie's knee bone was called osteomyelitis.

Every day for four months Mama and Papa rode the trolley to Mercy Hospital to visit Charlie. Every night for four months I waited for their return.

I was seven. The hospital rules posted in the front lobby said I was too young to visit my brother. That's why I stayed home, although Sister Cecilia did sneak me up to the third-floor children's ward to see Charlie one time. It was in January, right after Charlie's accident. She held her arm out to Mama as if she was guiding her through the halls, and hid me between the folds of the long, draping sleeve of her habit. She told me that two things were certain: if we could get past Mother Superior it would be a miracle, and the best medicine for Charlie was to know how much we all loved him.

Charlie was in a big room with other children, some older and some younger than his five years. I remember rushing over to the pillow covered with the familiar dark brown curls. "Charlie," I whispered, "I've come to take you home." I would help Mama and Papa take care of Charlie.

Charlie opened his eyes, and my heart sank at the same time. He looked all swallowed up in that big hospital bed with sides like a crib. I knew then that it would be a long time before Charlie would play Caddy with me and my best friend, Rosa. I just knew I would have to wait to play anything with Charlie, and I did.

Nobody ever told me why Sister Cecilia snuck me up to his room, but I think they were afraid Charlie would die. He was sick, really sick. The doctor operated on Charlie's knee, but the infection spread further down. The doctor wanted to amputate Charlie's leg above the knee. Papa told the doctor he would do anything he had to do to save Charlie's leg—the whole leg. That was when he and Mama found out about the doctor in Boston—if he couldn't help Charlie, then nobody could. Papa arranged for him to come to Johnstown and operate on Charlie's leg. Charlie ended up with a stiff knee, and he wore a shoe with a raised heel, but the doctor saved Charlie's whole leg.

Charlie finally came home at the end of April. At night he sat on the porch swing with me. He would point to the different constellations; then I would count the stars in them. We could hear Mama humming inside, and we thought the worst was over. It wasn't.

Everything started to change in May, after Mrs. DiLuso saw the shooting star. I remember she didn't even knock. I had just mopped the parlor floor for Mama when Mrs. DiLuso came rushing through the front door. With one step onto the wet floor, that four-foot-high, four-foot-around woman was all arms and legs, screeching wildly, "Oh, aaah, Ma-a-a-ma mia!" as she slid across the room.

One look from Mama and I bit the sides of my cheeks to keep from laughing at Mrs. DiLuso, the human cannonball. I stayed in the room long enough to see her come to a crashing halt, sprawled across the small table where I had sorted my postcard collection. Later Mama explained that Mrs. DiLuso had seen a star shooting across the sky above our neighborhood the night before. According to Mrs. DiLuso, who is very superstitious, it meant death or bad times for someone on Maple Avenue. There must have been a lot of shooting stars that night.

That same week Miss Penton, my teacher at Maple Avenue School, decided to fail the entire second grade. She insisted that there were students in our class who were not ready for third grade. If she failed one, she promised, she would fail everyone . . . and she did.

My papa was the only parent who wasn't afraid of Miss Penton's sharp tongue and puckered lips. He walked me to school one morning after the announcement, then made me wait in the hallway while he spoke with her. I heard him introduce himself. I didn't hear a word from Miss Penton. Papa went on to explain that he and Mama felt certain that I was prepared to attend third grade next year. He told her that I could add, subtract, multiply, use a cash register, make change, and write orders at our family store. I knew Miss Penton was angry; I heard her tapping a ruler on her desk the way she always did when someone crossed her. Miss Penton either ignored Papa's explanation, or did not hear a word he said while she tapped away. She simply told Papa that we Italian immigrants were in America now, and that our last name, Bandini, should be changed to Bandin. I couldn't hear what Papa said to Miss Penton, but my full name, Margo Bandini, remained on my report card. Papa won one battle, and Miss Penton won the other. The entire class, including Rosa and me, repeated the second grade.

That was four years ago, in 1929. Everything has changed on Maple Avenue. And to think I wasn't afraid—not then.

Chapter 2

<hr>

MAPLE AVENUE, 1933

Papa owned a shoe repair shop on Bedford Street. I often walked to work with him when there was no school. Every morning at six o'clock he crossed over the First Street Bridge, stopped to greet Mr. Bobb, who operated the train tower on the bridge, then walked the long trek past the steel mill. Papa stopped whistling and tipped his hat in respect as he passed St. John's Church. At the corner near the Swank Building, he started to whistle again, and continued until he reached the shop. As Papa unlocked the door he would pause to breathe in the balmy scents of leather and shoe polish. Then he'd turn on the lights, walk behind the counter, and put on his apron.

In the late afternoon, Papa closed the shop and walked past the bank on Main Street. There was a time when he would stop in the bank every Friday, just before closing. That was when he carried a small sack of money, proof of a busy week. He would smile as he proudly handed the sack over to the teller behind the counter. Sometimes Mr. Lockhard, the bank president, would smile back and shake Papa's hand. Not anymore. Now Papa walked by the bank jingling the small change in his pocket, sometimes carrying a basket of fresh fruit and vegetables.

Today I heard him tell Mama that Mr. Lockhard stood in the window of the bank yesterday. Papa tipped his hat, but Mr. Lockhard didn't seem to notice as he stared out at Main Street. He stopped shaking Papa's hand a long time ago, when Papa stopped carrying the money sack. Now Papa used the pocket change to pay our food bill.

Mr. Frappa, who owned a grocery store on Maple Avenue, kept a large black ledger of all the money people owed him. Every Friday Papa handed me our account book and sent me across the street to Mr. Frappa's store.

I knew we weren't poor. We had our house, a radio, and food. Rosa lived next door in her house. Her father was a steelworker.

One family in our neighborhood had to move away, one cold March day. It happened after the sheriff posted a sign on their front door—SHERIFF SALE, in big black letters. They had to leave everything behind except for the suitcases they carried, the clothes they wore, and their cat. I didn't tell Mama, but Rosa and I peeked into their basement window last week. It gave me the shivers to see their towels still hanging on the clothesline and the cat's box next to the stairs. Nobody knew where they went.

Mrs. DiLuso visited Mama tonight. Her visit seemed to carry a cloud of icy gloom, even though it was the middle of April. Cold chills ran down my spine as she reminded Mama that *il diavolo*, the devil, had brought the Depression to Maple Avenue the night she saw the shooting star. My fifth-grade teacher, Miss Dobson, said the Great Depression started in October of 1929, when the stock market crashed, banks closed, and people lost their money and their jobs. She even told us about wealthy men who had jumped out of windows because they had lost everything they owned.

Maple Avenue was snuggled between twin hill-sides. There were no wealthy people or fancy houses in my neighborhood. Our house was painted brown and had three stories. My bedroom was directly above our front porch and had two huge windows that met in the corner. From the front window I could see all of Maple Avenue, from the brickyard to the Acme Bakery. The side window looked out onto Rosa's front porch and, beyond that, St. Anthony's Church.

Tonight I could hear the steady squeak of the

front-porch swing as it rocked Mama and Papa back and forth. They often sat there at night while they talked.

"Margo, time for bed," called Mama.

"Good night, Mama and Papa."

I would leave the windows open. I didn't mind if the breeze came in, so long as the dark stayed out.

Chapter 3

MAPLE AVENUE NEWS

"Little brothers can be such a nuisance," announced Rosa.

I glanced back at Charlie and Rosa's younger brother, Michael.

"I heard that," Charlie yelled back.

"Well, then hurry," I called over my shoulder. "If the bell rings before we get to school, we'll all be staying after school, on a Friday afternoon."

The boys were walking a half block behind us. Charlie was showing Michael the gold pocket watch Papa had let him take to school today.

"I should remind you that Charlie is only one grade behind us," I told Rosa.

"I might remind *you* that as long as they're both wearing knickers and not long pants, they're still our little brothers," chided Rosa. "Where did he get that watch, anyway?"

"Papa was given that watch after the Great War. It belonged to a friend of his, a soldier Papa knew in the Yankee Division of the United States Army. They were stationed in France together. Papa received his United States citizenship papers while he was on the battlefield in the war. His friend died on that same battlefield. I'm not certain which Charlie is more fascinated by, the story behind the watch or the watch itself." I glanced over at Rosa, who came to a dead halt and stood there shaking her head.

"Your father let Charlie take something that valuable to school?"

I had to admit, even I was surprised. Papa kept that watch in the drawer of the server with his medal and his citizenship papers. Charlie was allowed to look at it, but Papa had never allowed him to take it out of the house before today.

"Maybe Papa thinks Charlie is growing up, even if he is in knickers." Teasing Rosa was something I loved to do. She was always so serious.

We made it to our seats as the bell rang. At lunchtime I saw Charlie showing the watch to a group of boys from my class. I started to wonder what Charlie had told everybody about the pocket watch. He was surrounded by fifth-grade girls at dismissal and didn't look the least bit shy about it.

"Catch me," I shouted as I tagged Rosa on the way home. It felt good to know the weekend was here.

Mama must have agreed, because Rosa and I sat and talked on my front porch until Papa came home for dinner. I didn't have to set the table or peel potatoes.

"Margo, take this to Mr. Frappa, please." Papa opened the screen door and handed me the account book, a dollar bill, and some change. "Call Charlie to dinner on your way home."

Charlie. Come to think of it, I hadn't seen him since we'd left school.

"He's probably at my house," answered Rosa. "I'll send him along. I have to go home for dinner, too."

I ran across the street to the grocery market. The bell on the door jingled as I walked in. Mr. Frappa was talking to Mrs. DiLuso and another customer. I walked over to the candy counter to wait my turn. My mouth watered, just looking at the peanut butter kisses and roasted peanuts.

"Gypsies . . . ," I could hear Mrs. DiLuso whisper, ". . . near Grandview Cemetery . . . the wealthy . . . steal food . . ."

The Gypsies had come to Johnstown before. Anything and everything that had been lost or stolen was blamed on their arrival. They were back, and so were the rumors. I put my nose up against the glass of the candy counter. I was sure that sweet smell was coming from the peanut butter kisses.

Mr. Frappa's grocery store had one of the few telephones in the neighborhood, and a radio, too. He always seemed to get the news first, then shared it with anyone who was interested. Mrs. DiLuso was always interested. She preferred to report her own version of the news to the neighborhood.

"Steal children . . . ," added the other customer.

Mr. Frappa smiled at me. He knew better than to interrupt and open his ledger while Mrs. DiLuso was there. I glanced up at the price board behind him.

Pork Chops, pound . . . . .15¢
Large Egg Plants .2 for 15¢
U.S. No. 1 Potatoes . . . . .Bushel 75¢
5 Lb. Sack Pastry Flour .9¢
Iceberg Lettuce, head . . . . .5¢
Fancy Sweet Peppers, each . . . . .1¢
Cocoanut Cup Cakes . . . . .4 for 5¢
Peanut Butter Kisses, pound . . . . .10¢

Mmmm, I could get a whole lot of peanut butter kisses for ten cents. I tried to think of something else. It was getting harder to wait for Mr. Frappa. I walked back to the door and looked for Charlie. I sure hoped he'd remembered to return Papa's watch before he'd gone out to play.

"Scusi, excuse me." Mrs. DiLuso was standing behind me.

I moved to let her and the other customer out the door.

"Ah, Margo. It's good to see you." Mr. Frappa was at my side.

I handed Mr. Frappa the money and our account book. He walked to the back of the counter and opened the ledger to our name. The page was filled with numbers. He counted the money I gave him, wrote the amount in his book and ours, then subtracted. We still owed him $12.75.

"Thank your mama and papa for me, Margo." He closed the books. "What news do you bring me today?"

I had to smile. The fun was about to begin. Miss Dobson's father owned the local newspaper. She'd bring the daily edition to school every morning and use the first ten minutes of geography class to discuss the news. Mr. Frappa and I enjoyed a good game of news tag at least once a week.

"Miss Dobson told us today that the drought in Oklahoma is so bad, the topsoil blows away in the wind." I was proud of myself. Mr. Frappa had been a teacher somewhere near Pittsburgh. He'd returned to Johnstown to tend the family store after his school was closed down because they couldn't pay the teachers.

"Did you know that entire families are leaving their Oklahoma farms and moving west to find work in California? They call them Okies," he told me. Mr. Frappa always got the last word in.

Last year he used the price board as a news board to keep track of Amelia Earhart's flight across the Atlantic, to inform his customers that the New York Yankees had won the World Series, and to let them know that Franklin Delano Roosevelt had beaten Herbert Hoover in the presidential election. Sometimes his store felt like a classroom. He always made the neighborhood children count their own change. He even gave me a postcard for my collection. It had a picture of the Empire State Building on it, the world's tallest building.

"Charlie was in today. He—"

"Charlie! Dinner! Oh boy, I'm in trouble." I shouted a good-bye to Mr. Frappa as I ran out the door and headed home. *Please, Charlie, be home.* When I got back to the house, Mama and Papa were waiting at the dinner table.

"Come, Margo. Dinner is getting cold. Charlie should be along soon," said Mama.

I was relieved that they didn't ask me if I'd looked for him. It took him a little longer to get around, and he often arrived home just as we sat down to dinner.

But Charlie had really done it this time. Mama never said a word all through dinner, and kept glancing at the door. Papa asked me about my school day, but I could tell by the way he kept looking at Mama that he was wondering about Charlie, too.

"Margo, you wash the dishes, and I will clear the table," said Mama as we finished eating.

I knew it was not the right time to share my thoughts about the unfairness of it all. Charlie had missed dinner, and now Mama was doing his job.

I finished washing the dishes and turned to see Papa standing at our front door. "Margo, where did you go to look for Charlie?"

I remembered our account book in my pocket and handed it to him. "Papa, I was talking to Mr. Frappa and didn't have time to look for Charlie. Maybe Rosa forgot to tell him to come home, too." The troubled look in Papa's eyes made me add, "I'm sure he took very good care of your pocket watch, Papa." I opened the drawer to pull out the watch as proof. The watch wasn't there. I didn't even stop to close the drawer.

"Papa, I'll go find Charlie," I called. The screen door slammed shut behind me. Maybe Rosa was right—little brothers in knickers were a nuisance. Charlie was in trouble for not returning the watch when he got home from school, and now I was in trouble for not finding him.

Chapter 4

CHARLIE

Rosa's front door was closed. I knocked hard. No answer. I could hear shouting inside. That seemed to happen often at Rosa's house. I knocked harder. Rosa came to the front door, opened it wide enough to squeeze through, and closed it behind her. She had been crying.

"Are you okay, Rosa?"

She looked at me and swallowed hard. "The steel mill cut my father's work hours again. He's working one day a week now. My mother insists on taking in sewing and laundry. I could help, too. But my father won't let us. He believes it's a man's job to support his family, and that if my mother and I have to work, then he has failed us all. He wants us to move to Buffalo, New York. He heard there's work there for any man who wants it."

"Oh, Rosa, you wouldn't kid me, would you?

We've been friends all our lives." I tried to keep my voice steady and to act grown up. But the thought of my best friend moving away made me feel like a lost little kid.

"My father said he won't wait for the sheriff to post a sign on our door. He said we'll leave before anybody comes to force us out. We don't have the money to pay our mortgage."

A loud crash from inside quieted both of us. Michael came running down the narrow sidewalk that led from their backyard. He suddenly looked much younger than nine. His beet-red face was smudged with grime and streaks of tears.

His voice cracked. "I—I had to do something to stop the shouting. I won't move to Buffalo."

Rosa looked through the window of the front door. Her mother was picking up the scattered pieces of a glass vase.

"Michael, I think you'd better stay with us for a while. We can sit on Margo's front porch." Rosa looked at me the same way she did when I had that rare licorice whip and was debating whether or not I should share it.

"I'm not so sure you want to do that," I said. "I'm in just as much trouble as you are. Michael, if Charlie isn't with you, then where is he? He never came home for dinner."

"I haven't seen him since, uh, since after school."

Mama had a way of knowing when I wasn't telling the truth. All she had to say was, "Margo, your chin is growing." It worked every time. There was something in the way Michael rolled his big blue eyes and bit his lower lip that made me suspect he knew more than he was telling. But I couldn't wait any longer. If Papa didn't have the pocket watch back soon, Charlie and I would both be punished.

"Look, if you see Charlie, tell him he'd better get home fast with Papa's watch."

"Sorry, Margo." Rosa pulled Michael to her side. "We'd come with you to look for Charlie, but . . ."

"It's okay." Something deep inside me stirred. I remembered what it was like to want to protect a little brother. I turned away just in time to see Mrs. DiLuso walking up the steps of my front porch. For once I was thankful for her timing. She would occupy Mama and Papa while I found my little brother.

Charlie was an altar server at St. Anthony's Church, and had become friendly with some of the boys who lived at the church's orphanage. I walked to the back of the orphanage where a group of boys were playing kickball. Charlie wasn't there, and nobody had seen him all day.

I ran to the coal heap. It was nothing more than a fenced-in piece of land where workmen poured the used coal ashes from the brickyard ovens. Charlie often took a small tin bucket there, to collect the chunks of coal left in the pile. Mama was so angry with him the first time he came home covered in black that she made him promise to deliver anything he found to the family with the cat. That was before the SHERIFF SALE sign went up and they were forced to leave their home. I wondered if Mama knew that, since they'd moved, Charlie traded the coal chunks for pieces of candy at Frappa's. I swore that if Charlie didn't show up soon, I'd tell Mama myself.

A horn beeped outside a neighbor's house across the street. A group of kids deserted a game of dodgeball in the alley to examine the shiny black car. I crossed the street to see if Charlie was with them. One of the kids said he'd seen Charlie in Frappa's Grocery Store after school. That was all anybody knew.

I turned and ran back down the street. The sun was setting when I got to Frappa's. The store was dark and the door was locked. I wished I had listened more closely when Mr. Frappa had mentioned he'd seen Charlie. I ran to the brickyard.

The corner lot between the factory and the neighborhood houses supported an elevated train track. A tunnel under the tracks led from the lot into another open area. Rosa had seen the older boys smoking in there last week. I called through the tunnel, "Cha-ar-lie. Charlie, you answer me right now." But there was no answer.

I couldn't help feeling that this was not good. My stomach flip-flopped as my mind raced back in time. The last time Charlie had missed dinner was the evening Mama and Papa rushed him to the hospital. I shook my head and tried to erase the terrible memory. I stomped my foot and let out a groan that echoed through the tunnel, then turned and looked up Maple Avenue one last time as I headed toward home.

Everybody on Maple Avenue knew Charlie. He'd stop a game of kickball to help carry a neighbor's groceries, then turn around and get into mischief in the wink of an eye. Mr. Bobb had to chase him off the arches of the bridge one day. Charlie and Michael had wanted to see who could climb the highest without getting caught. There was quite an uproar the day Charlie snuck a garter snake into school. The principal pulled me out of Miss Dobson's class and made me walk Charlie home.

Here I was again. When Charlie got into mischief, I got into trouble. It was a good thing Charlie wasn't a twin. Lola Nola, a girl in my class, had too many brothers, including a set of twins. Everybody called them Double and Trouble. Lola came to school one time with a fat lip. She had been punished for not watching her younger brother. He was caught stealing apples from . . . Stealing? *Stealing?*

I stopped dead in my tracks. "Stealing?" I said

out loud. My mind raced back in time again, to Mr. Frappa's store and to what I had heard. What had the customer said about the Gypsies stealing children? Mrs. DiLuso would know, and I knew where to find her.

Chapter 5

THE SEARCH

By the time I got home, my heart felt as if it would pop right out of my chest. Papa met me at the front door.

The words were caught in the back of my throat. I was afraid to hear myself say them. "I—I can't find him, Papa. Nobody has seen Charlie since Mr. Frappa's store. He was there after school, then left."

I glanced at Mrs. DiLuso, who was shaking her head and beating at her chest with a clenched fist. "*Il diavolo*, again. The Gypsies have your Charlie."

"*Stai zitto*, keep quiet!" Papa's dark brown eyes were like daggers. Dead silence followed.

My papa never talked to Mama like that. People loved my papa. He helped everyone. The farmers always went into the shoe shop to see Papa. He would fix their shoes even if they didn't have money. They would trade a basket of fruit and vegetables for a pair of heels. Papa would bring the basket home, and what Mama didn't use we gave to the neighbors. Everybody loved my papa. He never talked like that to anyone.

Mama's eyes filled with tears. I wasn't sure if she was embarrassed by Papa's outburst, or if she believed Mrs. DiLuso.

"Margo, think hard," said Papa in a much gentler tone. "Why would Charlie not come home? Where could he be?"

"It's your watch, Papa. He didn't return it to the drawer. He had it when I saw him, but that was on our way home from school. Papa, what if one of the Gypsies saw Charlie with the gold watch? Charlie would never let anyone take it away from him. He knows what that watch means to you. What if the Gypsies took Charlie and the watch? They steal chickens and *children*—everybody knows that." I looked at Mrs. DiLuso, certain she would agree. Her head was down and her eyes were closed. Was she praying, or was she expecting Papa to yell again?

"I heard those rumors in the shop today," said Papa. "Officer Franks stopped in to pick up his shoes. The only report of anything missing is a crate of chickens that fell off the back of a farmer's truck on his way in from Somerset County."

Mrs. DiLuso looked straight at Papa. "Aaah, so

we still have missing chickens, a missing boy, and now a missing watch. Three. Bad luck comes in threes."

Papa's hands were clenched at his sides. He looked at Mama, shook his head, and said, "I will find Charlie." He was out the front door before we could say another word.

I caught up with Papa as he knocked on Rosa's door and asked for her father. Mr. Meglio helped Papa round up the other neighbors, and they went looking for my brother. Rosa was at my side. Maple Avenue echoed with shouts of "Charlie! Charlie Bandini!"

It looked like a neighborhood game of hide-and-seek, with everybody searching and calling his name. Charlie was the best at hiding. I just hoped he'd shout "Base!" real soon. It was getting dark.

A Letter to Mrs. Roosevelt

C. COCO DE YOUNG

Set during the Great Depression, A Letter to Mrs. Roosevelt *is a heartwarming story of an eleven-year-old girl's courageous attempt to save her family's home.*

ABOUT THE BOOK

The Great Depression has disrupted the safe and secure life that Margo Bandini has grown to enjoy in the small town of Johnstown, Pennsylvania, where she lives with her parents and younger brother. In school, Margo has studied Black Thursday and the Domino Effect. But the dark days take on a new meaning when she comes home from school and sees a Sheriff Sale sign on her house. Desperate to save her family from economic despair, Margo writes to Eleanor Roosevelt for help. When she receives an unexpected reply, Margo scores a victory for her family and learns the true meaning of brotherhood.

IN THE CLASSROOM

A Letter to Mrs. Roosevelt is a story about *brotherhood, courage and fear, pride,* and *family and relationships.* The vivid portrayal of the period and the heartwarming reality of a family's struggle to survive economic devastation will help students understand this dark period in America's history.

The powerful themes, the courage of the eleven-year-old main character, and the strong sense of story make the novel ideal for a novel study or read-aloud. This guide offers activities for using the novel to connect language arts, social studies, health, and careers.

PRE-READING ACTIVITY

Eleanor Roosevelt was a champion of human rights. Read aloud Article I from the Universal Declaration of Human Rights: "All human beings are born free and equal in dignity and rights. They are endowed with reason and conscience and should act towards one another in a spirit of brotherhood." Discuss with the class the meaning of different ways of showing brotherhood. Then ask students to find an article in the local newspaper about someone who has demonstrated brotherhood, summarize the article in one sentence, and display their sentences on a bulletin board.

THEMATIC CONNECTIONS

✎ **Brotherhood**—Discuss how Mr. and Mrs. Bandini show brotherhood. Who else in their neighborhood displays brotherhood? Cite evidence in the novel that Miss Dobson, Margo's teacher, is dedicated to helping others. How can we carry on Eleanor Roosevelt's "spirit of brotherhood"?

✎ **Courage and Fear**—Have the class discuss Margo's greatest fears. How do her parents help her deal with her fears? When does Margo show courage? Ask students to discuss what they think Margo's most courageous act is. Why does Mr. Bandini think his Victory Medal will give Margo courage? Ask students to think about what they would say to Margo if they were presenting her with a medal for courage.

✎ **Family and Relationships**—Compare Rosa's family to the Bandini family. How does each family deal with the economic strain of the Depression? What could Rosa's father learn from Mr. Bandini? Describe how each member of the Bandini family pitches in to help when things get tough. How do you know that Mama and Papa Bandini have respect for each other?

✎ **Pride**—What does the phrase *swallow your pride* mean? How do the people in the novel have to swallow their pride? Who has the most difficult time swallowing pride? What does the phrase *false sense of pride* mean? How do Mr. and Mrs. Bandini instill pride in Margo and Charley?

INTERDISCIPLINARY CONNECTIONS

Language Arts—It was said of Eleanor Roosevelt that she would rather light candles than curse the darkness. Engage the class in a discussion of the meaning of this quotation. Ask students to write a letter that Eleanor Roosevelt might have written to Margo commending her for "lighting a candle."

Social Studies—The Great Depression began on October 24, 1929, a day called Black Thursday. Ask students to research the causes and effects of Black Thursday. Then ask them to write a front-page article that might have appeared in the Johnstown, Pennsylvania, newspaper.

Eleanor Roosevelt is credited with changing the role of the First Lady. Ask students to research Mrs. Roosevelt's activities during her years as First Lady. Then have them list the activities and accomplishments of First Ladies since Eleanor Roosevelt. Of these women, which do you think Mrs. Roosevelt would most admire? Which would most admire Eleanor Roosevelt?

Health—Charley has osteomyelitis and is hospitalized for four months. Franklin D. Roosevelt was stricken with polio and confined to a wheelchair. Find out the cause of each disease and the treatments. Find out when the cure for polio was discovered. Have students locate information about the hospital in Warm Springs, Georgia, where Franklin Roosevelt went for treatment.

Careers—Miss Dobson tells Margo that she is a good writer and should consider a career in journalism. Have students find different job opportunities in journalism and places in their state or region where they can study journalism.

Creative Drama—Have the class watch the movie *Annie* and compare the setting of the movie to the setting of *A Letter to Mrs. Roosevelt*. Who is Margo Bandini's Daddy Warbucks? Divide the class into small groups. Ask each group to prepare a scene in which Margo Bandini meets Annie after the Roosevelts have touched their lives.

VOCABULARY/USE OF LANGUAGE

The vocabulary in the novel isn't difficult, but students should record words that are unfamiliar and try to define them, using the context of the story. Such words may include *superstitious* (p. 4), *ledger* (p. 7), *mortgage* (p. 18), *inauguration* (p. 27), and *collateral* (p. 54).

RELATED TITLES
BY THEME AND TOPIC

Cat Running
Zilpha Keatley Snyder
- Great Depression
- Courage
- Family
- Pride
Grades 4–6 / 0-440-41152-1

Lily's Crossing
Patricia Reilly Giff
- Fear
- Courage
- Family
- Brotherhood
Grades 4–6 / 0-440-41453-9

Moving Mama to Town
Ronder Thomas Young
- Great Depression
- Family
- Pride
- Courage
Grades 4–6 / 0-440-41455-5

Purely Rosie Pearl
Patricia A. Cochrane
- Great Depression
- Family
- Courage
Grades 4–6 / 0-440-41344-3

UNIVERSAL DECLARATION OF HUMAN RIGHTS

On the Web, sponsored by the United Nations
High Commissioner for Human Rights.
www.unhchr.ch/udhr/lang/eng.htm

ELEANOR ROOSEVELT NATIONAL HISTORIC SITE WEB SITE

Provides information about the Hyde Park,
New York, home of the former First Lady.
www.nps.gov/elro/elrohome.html

JOHNSTOWN, PENNSYLVANIA, HISTORIC INFORMATION WEB SITE

Gives lots of information on the setting of
A Letter to Mrs. Roosevelt.
www.johnstownpa.com/history.html

NEW DEAL NETWORK

Sponsored by the Franklin and Eleanor Roosevelt Institute
and the Institute for Learning Technologies,
this Web site contains information on the New Deal,
Great Depression, and WPA.
www.ilt.columbia.edu/projects/new_deal.html

Prepared by Pat Scales, Director of Library Services,
South Carolina Governor's School for the Arts and Humanities,
Greenville

ABOUT THE AUTHOR

C. Coco De Young grew up in Johnstown, Pennsylvania. Her first novel, *A Letter to Mrs. Roosevelt,* is the winner of the Sixth Annual Marguerite de Angeli Prize for a first middle-grade novel. This inspiring tale of a young girl's fight to save her family home during the Great Depression is based on the true stories that have been handed down over generations in the author's family.

Ms. De Young's grandfather grew up during the Depression. When his family's well-being was threatened, he wrote a letter to Mrs. Roosevelt, and his plea for help was answered. Ms. De Young's grandfather is believed to be one of the first people in Johnstown to receive a loan through President Roosevelt's Home Owners Loan Corporation, a part of the New Deal relief program.

Ms. De Young is a graduate of Seton Hill College in Greensburg, Pennsylvania. An elementary school teacher for several years, she lives in Ridgefield, Connecticut, with her husband and four children. Although she no longer lives in Pennsylvania, the people of Johnstown are in her heart, and she will always admire the courage of its wonderful citizens.

VISIT OUR WEB SITE!

TeachersatRandom
A Web site for K–12 teachers and librarians

www.randomhouse.com/teachers

FREE TEACHER'S GUIDES
- More than 100 exclusive guides
- Developed by leading educators
- Great curriculum tie-ins
- Dozens of fun classroom activities
- Innovative thematic and interdisciplinary connections

FREE AUTHOR AND ILLUSTRATOR PROFILES
- Over 100 extensive biographies
- Fun facts—favorite hobbies, inspiration for writing, and more

NUMEROUS INDEXES
- Titles identified by theme, discipline, author, and grade level
- High-interest books that appeal to reluctant readers

LINKS TO
TeensatRandom
KidsatRandom
Web resources

For additional activities and Internet resources for the four books in this exclusive teacher's edition, visit us online.